Every Woman Needs

a Praying Man

PAT SIMMONS

Every Woman
Needs A Praying Man
By
Pat Simmons

ISBN-13: 978-1523821273
ISBN-10: 1523821272

Content/copy editor: Rahab Mugwanja/Giggle Girl
Editing Services
Proofreader: Ashley Clarke/A.K. Clarke Editing
Beta Reader: Stacey Jefferson
Cover design: Nat Mara/Bookaholic Fiverr.com
Author photo: Angie Knost Photography

Dedication

To those of you who need a touch from God. Stay prayerful.

Philippians 4:6: *Be careful for nothing, but in everything by prayer and supplication with thanksgiving, let your requests be known unto God.*

Acknowledgments

None of my stories could have depth without my sources sharing their valuable time speaking with me or answering my emails. I found aspects of billboard advertising fascinating, so I reached out to chat with Don Barner, President BillBoard Connection.

Readers' Praise for Pat Simmons

5 Stars. "Heartwarming. A wonderful Christian novel about true love. I love the way the author intertwined scriptures into the story."—Angela on *A Baby for Christmas*

5 Stars. "Pat Simmons did it again!! This book is full of love, life lessons and most importantly Christ. I love how Pat interjects the word/voice of God into this story and all of her books." –Joyce N on *A Noelle for Nathan*

5 Stars. "This was another great read by Pat Simmons….I also love how my spirit is always lifted and encouraged after reading her books." –Book Diva on *The Confession*

5 Stars. "Wow, this book was so inspirational. It had so much to it but what I loved was learning about a Christian Christmas." –A reader on *A Christian Christmas* (Book 1 Andersen Brothers)

5 Stars. "How romantic for a man of God to be drawn to a woman because of her heart to God, to be turned on by her praise to God? David saw her, fell hard, and pursued his 'Hart' and won. I loved this story."—T. Baker on *A Woman After David's Heart* (Book 2 Andersen Brothers)

5 Stars. "Wow, I laughed and cried and that was hard because I was on Jury Duty and sitting in the front. Be careful where you read them because these books make you want to rejoice in the Lord when you least expect." – A reader on *Christmas Greetings*

5 Stars. "Every character has their own interesting storyline. Simmons developed the characters so that I was drawn into their stories. I could feel every emotion. I laughed, cried, and wondered with each of them. It kept me glued to the pages. This was my first time reading Simmons's work, but I look forward to others." –Donnica Copeland, APOOO BookClub, Sista Talk Book Club, *Not Guilty of Love*

Chapter One

Monica Wyatt swallowed, hoping to calm her nerves as she gripped the steering wheel. Her unseen enemy was back like a powerful jaguar locked on its target—her. She couldn't explain the fear devouring her on a path she had driven on since she received her license at sixteen, but self-preservation was what mattered.

Although she had just maneuvered her Mazda 6 into the fast lane on I-170 in North St. Louis County, something within her shouted, "Get off the highway now!" As her arms began to tingle, she veered her car into the center lane without using her turn signal. "Hurry," she mumbled.

Other vehicles were fast-approaching. Monica dove into the slow lane and skidded to a stop onto the shoulder, almost clipping the rear end of a pickup truck.

With labored breath and a racing heart, she rested, more like collapsed, her forehead on the steering wheel. Her heart thrashed against her chest as if it was clawing its way out to abandon ship. Her eyes blurred, so she closed her lids. Whatever was going on, she didn't have time for this, not when she had an interview for a job she desperately needed to snag. She was only three miles, maybe four, away from her exit, yet she felt like her destination was hours away. Maybe she was about to have a heart attack. But she was only thirty-one. "God, help me."

She coaxed herself to get a grip, and wasn't referring to the steering wheel. When someone tapped on her window, Monica would have ejected from her seat if not for her seat belt. Startled, her eyes popped open. A dark-skinned man came into focus. He looked to be about her age. His eyebrows were as silky black as his mustache. If he was her compact mirror, her anxiety was reflected on his face, marring his perfection.

"Are you okay?" he mouthed.

Cracking the window an inch, Monica shook her head at the same time her mouth uttered, "Yes."

"Which one is it? Are you having car problems or is there a medical emergency?" Without waiting for her response, he began to scold her about her erratic driving. "I wasn't far behind you when you pulled that stunt. This isn't a speedway." Upset didn't begin to describe him.

She groaned at his depiction. "I was scared, okay!" she snapped as a tear fell. "I'm all right."

"You don't seem all right," he argued. "Can you open the door? Let me help you."

"I may be having a crisis, but I'm not crazy. I don't know you!" Her hands still trembled. The stranger looked built under his black coat. *Stop ogling.* She didn't envision starting her Friday morning like this.

"You have to get off the side of the road. It's not safe." His brown eyes pleaded with her.

"I need just a few minutes," she lied. It would take a couple of hours to analyze what happened, but she wasn't computing numbers as a market researcher; she was dealing with something she couldn't see. "I'll be fine."

"I'm talking about me. It's not safe." He tilted his head over his shoulder. "There's a pack of semis coming at us, and I happen to like my life." Despite the lines creasing his forehead, he actually smirked, which made her chuckle. He, being her temporary distraction, was calming her nerves.

"I'm sorry to put you in harm's way. Please get back in your car." She didn't want to be responsible for his death. No, it wasn't a good day for anyone to die, especially her.

A casualty of downsizing at a non-profit health organization three months earlier and endless job searches, Monica had planned to wow this prospective employer with her skills. She hoped beyond reason to be offered the position on the spot. *It wasn't going to happen now.*

"Listen…I don't even know your name?" he shouted as cars roared past them. Before she could open her mouth, the man gritted his teeth. "Fine. I'll have it my way," he said and disappeared.

Whatever. She noted the highway, which seemed like an endless ocean. The tsunami of fear began to descend on her again, causing her hands to tremble and perspiration to dot her upper lip. Even her deodorant was losing its battle.

"God, what is happening to me? I've got to snap out of this." Monica Wyatt wasn't a wimp. Her older brother had made sure of it. While taking deep breaths to regain control, she glanced in the rear view mirror and groaned. Apparently stubborn, the stranger was still there.

Suddenly, sirens pierced her ears until they blocked her escape. The Good Samaritan was nowhere in sight. She sighed and braced herself for round two of mortification. If television crews showed up, she was done. Maybe, she would die today from embarrassment.

For the next twenty minutes, Monica answered the medic's questions. "No, I'm not on medication…No, I don't want to be transported for evaluation…Yes, I felt tingling in my limbs, so I pulled over…Yes, I'm fine now…No, I don't have any insurance," she told them, handing over her driver's license. "No, you don't have to call someone."

Once she convinced the first responders she didn't need medical attention, they said she could go on her merry way. The problem: it was too late to make the best first impression on her interview. That was enough to make her depressed. But she wasn't one to waddle in self-pity.

Starting the ignition, Monica held her head high with feigned confidence and drove her car at a crawl to the nearest exit. In a daze, she returned to her Olivette condo, replaying the fiasco she'd caused on the highway. She undressed and climbed back in bed. Maybe when she awoke, it will all have been a nightmare.

An hour or so later, her best friend's ringtone chimed. Monica started to ignore the call, but decided to answer. Veronica Lee was pulling for her to get the job too. "Hey."

"Uh-oh. Sounds like you didn't get the position. Oh, I'm so sorry."

"Me too." She blinked back moisture as she scanned her spacious master bedroom, decorated in warm fall colors of greens, rust, and burgundy. If she didn't get a job soon, her condo would be back on the market. "I never made it. Girl, I freaked out again...paramedics and the police—"

"Hold up and back up! What do you mean *again*?" Veronica's high-pitched voice was proof she was alarmed.

Oops. Monica realized she never told her friend about the first incident which had happened a few weeks earlier. "Ah, well, I was leaving the hair salon, minding my own business..." She frowned as she racked her brain on how to describe it. "One minute, I was singing along with the radio. The next, out of nowhere, I felt heart palpitations, became lightheaded." She paused. "I had this sensation as if I was detached from reality like an out-of-body experience. It freaked me out, so I cursed and in the same breath prayed."

"I'm sure that didn't work, but you never told me. Why?"

Licking her lips, Monica stalled. "That's not something I want to relive, even with my best friend."

Veronica was quiet. Did she think Monica was going crazy? "Hmm-mmm, so nobody knows about this, not even your mom?"

"Definitely not!"

"Well, if Ms. Ollie doesn't know, maybe I should be the snitch."

"Don't you dare," Monica warned. She'd moved across town to have some distance between her and her parents who still thought of her as their baby girl, literally. If Ollie Wyatt knew, she would have an ambulance waiting outside Monica's door. "Until I can figure this out, no need to worry her."

"You know I wouldn't say a word. So is that how you felt today?" Veronica asked in a no-nonsense tone. "I'll look up symptoms."

Twirling a strand of hair around her finger, she gave it some thought while she heard her friend tapping on keyboards in the background. "I wasn't lightheaded, but my arms were tingling. I was feeling kinda out of control, mostly afraid."

"*Mmm-hmm*. Sounds like you had panic attacks. I'm on this website called—"

"No, thanks. I just lived through it. I don't need to read it." Monica pulled the covers back, padded across the carpet to her gas fireplace, and turned it on. This amenity had been the selling point when she purchased the condo two years ago.

"Okay, maybe you need to go to the doctor," Veronica suggested.

"You think?" she said sarcastically. "I don't have a job, remember? No health insurance. I can't even afford the premiums on the government subsidized coverage. I have a new car, a house note…" Thinking about her finances was exhausting. Leaning on the mantle, she stared into the fire. *Panic attacks*, she repeated her friend's unconfirmed diagnosis.

If a person ate too much, they became overweight; ingest too much sugar—cavities; tanning stations—skin cancer; panic attacks? She drew a blank.

Professionally, Monica dealt with numbers as a data analyst. Things always added up. This wasn't logical. There was no family history. Her parents seemed normal and were rather healthy. She never knew them to take more than an aspirin. Her older brother, Alexander, was too smart for his own good. So why her and why now? "All I know is it came out of nowhere."

"Which is why you need to call and see if you can reschedule the interview." Although Monica balked at the idea, her friend didn't back down. "What do you have to lose? Tell him you had an emergency, which I'm sure the 911 tapes will verify. At least you had the mind to call for help."

"I didn't. This guy stopped to help." His presence had temporarily calmed her. "He had the kindest eyes."

"Was he cute?"

"Put it this way, if I wasn't in distress, I would have flirted," Monica joked and flopped back onto her bed. But she would never forget his face or the concern on it.

"Hmm. Never know where you will meet your future husband." She giggled.

"I hope not on the side of the road. Anyway, I'll keep job searching on LinkedIn."

"What about the girl who referred you? Can you get a hold of her to run interference? The job is paying way too much for you to say, 'forget it'," Veronica harped until she wore Monica down.

"Maybe you're causing me these panic attacks."

"Not funny. Listening to what you went through is scary." Veronica cleared her throat. "I can always show up, say I was you and—"

"Oh, no you don't. The last time you did me a favor, it cost me a parking ticket."

"Good. I'm glad we reached this understanding. Call the company and get back to me. Bye."

She knew job interview protocol. Monica blew it, but to keep Veronica from hounding her, she retrieved a copy of the email that listed the company's contact number. "Here goes a waste of time." Taking in a deep breath, she exhaled and called. "Mr. Dyson please."

With two sisters and a mother like Earline, Tyson Graham knew better than to leave a female stranded on the road—a looker or otherwise. The woman, even in her frightened state, was beautiful with her full lips and slanted eyes, even if they were dazed. She left him no choice but to call for medical backup. Once EMTs were within range, he took off free from guilt.

Now, minutes after arriving late at the office, he was informed the leading candidate for the marketing research position at Tyson & Dyson Communications, LLC didn't bother to show up. "Great," Tyson mumbled to Mrs. Coates, his elderly administrative assistant who also happened to babysit him and his two sisters when they were babes in diapers. For him, thirty-six years ago.

What a major disappointment since the other applicants' skills dulled in comparison to this candidate's. She had almost ten years of working at a non-profit in market databases. Her type of experience was priceless. Maybe the woman's no-show was for the best, considering Tyson wasn't in the mood to be cordial to anyone.

"Hey, how was the conference?" Reginald "Reggie" Dyson, his business partner, asked as Tyson rounded the corner toward his office.

"Impressive. We're definitely going in the right direction, securing our out-of-home media advertising to include taxi tops and bus shelters." He paused to unwrap his wool scarf from his neck and unbutton his coat. "But the money is still in the billboards and the new digital ones would make David Copperfield's illusions look like a kid's game," he joked. "It ain't grandma's advertising anymore."

"Hey," Mrs. Coates yelled from the lobby. "I'm somebody's grandma and great-grandma. Ain't nothing wrong with being a grandma."

Reggie shook his head and grinned. "You started it."

"Tell me about it." Tyson continued to his office. Standing outside his door, he smirked. "Have you ever seen a great-grandma with jet-black hair?"

"Nope." Reggie snickered and headed toward the company's kitchen/lounge that Mrs. Coates stocked and transformed to what she called a café boutique.

"I heard that too!" This time the woman was standing at the end of the hallway, glaring at them. "Wait until your AARP card comes in the mail, then you'll go by the beauty supply store to buy some black hair dye, too."

Tyson knew better than to tangle with Mrs. Coates. She had been with him and Reggie since day one, which was five years ago, not for the money per se, but to escape babysitting those grandbabies. Go figure. One thing was for sure, if they ever relocated or renovated their office in this historic building, he would demand better-insulated walls.

He and Reggie were old buddies who lost touch after high school, but reconnected eight years earlier while enrolled in an MBA program at St. Louis University. Despite Tyson's education at an Ivy League Brown University and Reggie graduating from the prestigious HBCU Hampton University, they both found themselves disenchanted with advancement of blacks in higher management positions in Corporate America.

After two years of grant writing and networking, the two invested in outdoor advertising or out-of-home advertising (OOH), which seemed to be the most lucrative when it came to bringing in the big bucks. To them, in-home advertising, such as circulars, were old school. As the chief executive officer, Tyson was the driving force behind thinking and doing business outside the box. Reggie was the chief financial officer and watched their money with his undergrad degree in accounting.

He refocused on business. The demonstration at the conference was impressive, but he and Reggie were psyched about digital technology being more than a pretty picture. The webinar they were anticipating would showcase a digital billboard in Peru, which fused with technology to pull moisture from the air with a mechanism installed inside the billboard to create about twenty gallons of water a day to a drought-stricken village in Lima.

Tyson signed into his email account only to learn the webinar had been rescheduled. He pounded his fist on the desk. Could his day get any worse? First, his plane from North Carolina was delayed, then a deranged damsel nearly got him killed on the side of a highway.

He rubbed his forehead. Nothing was going his way. Leaning back in his chair, he spun around and was drawn into the light snow shower outside his office window. His mind drifted back to the crazy woman, and the haunted expression on her face. Was she on drugs or intoxicated? Under different circumstances, he would have been intrigued by her eyes—a rich brown, but the fear in them was intense and he was afraid for her, not knowing what kind of help she needed.

"Hey, Ty," Reggie said, walking into his office without knocking. "You want some good news?"

Swerving his chair around, Tyson faced him. "Yep. Whatcha got?"

"The applicant who didn't show up just called. She apologized, said she had an emergency, and wanted to reschedule if we hadn't hired anybody." He grinned.

Tyson nodded with a smirk of his own. "I'm sure you accommodated her request."

"You know it. She'll be here Monday at ten, so don't be late!"

"Yeah, right. You're the one who's going to Florida for the weekend to see Tracee. Make sure you make it back." Tyson chuckled, wondering how his friend was going to survive this newfound long-distance relationship. The two friends had made a pact to always put business first. He hoped Tracee wouldn't cause them to add an addendum. Clearing his head, he dismissed unnecessary worry. If Reggie slipped, Tyson would be there to pick up the slack. Nothing would distract him from the success of their company, not even a woman.

Chapter Two

Monica said two quick prayers Monday morning: one that she would get the job and the second that she would get there without delay. She climbed into her car and gunned the engine before leaving her condo complex. Unafraid, she exited on I-170 and cruised with the flow of traffic. When she passed the shoulder where her meltdown had taken place, she lifted an eyebrow and smirked. "Not today."

She pulled into the parking lot of Tyson & Dyson Communications fifteen minutes early and entered the lobby. A petite woman with short black hair and gray eyebrows greeted her with a big smile. "Good morning."

"Hi, I'm—"

"Monica!" Solae Kavanaugh said, rounding a corner. The woman who was about the same age as her had been a godsend. Actually, their chance meeting had been a result of a visit to a random church as part of a New Year's resolution between her and Veronica, but her friend bailed out. During a potty break in the ladies' room, she noticed the slender woman could be a stand-in for Nia Long.

After Monica complimented the mother and daughter on their matching outfits, Solae had introduced herself, eyeing Monica's visitor badge. Things got interesting when Solae learned her last name.

"I have Wyatts in my family. I knew I felt a kindred spirit." And just like that, Solae coerced out of Monica her parents' names, age, and where she lived and worked.

"I'm between jobs. I got laid off recently. I guess there isn't a high demand for a marketing researcher with ten years experience." She did her best not to sound discouraged.

Solae's face brightened and she grinned. "God is good. The company I work for is expanding. You might want to give them a call."

They both dug into their purses and pulled out business cards.

"Wait a minute, Hershey," Solae said quietly to her daughter, who was vying for her attention, before turning back to Monica. "I'll definitely put in a good word. After all, we could be cousins, and please come back to our services." They left the ladies' room together, but headed in opposite directions. Excited about the lead, Monica hadn't heard a word of the sermon.

Seeing Solae again made her feel guilty about skipping church the day before, especially after she told the woman she would return.

"You've got this." Solae's eyes twinkled as she gave a thumbs up. She stepped back and the waiting receptionist ushered Monica into a conference room. It was medium-sized with a rich dark executive table for at least eight. Her shoes sunk into plush tan carpet. A cabinet countertop laden with treats was on one end of the table. A flat screen hanging on the opposite wall seemed to act as the focal point for the head of the table.

"Please feel free to grab a water, if you like," the receptionist said before closing the door behind her.

After removing her coat, she did, and took a seat. The door opened and a tall muscular man filled the room with a commanding presence. He was clean-shaven and had a boyish look about his face. His hair was faded on the sides with short twists on top—trendy. Although he was definitely a head-turner, he reminded Monica of her ex. There was no crush coming from her.

He extended his hand. "Monica, it's nice to meet you. I'm

Reginald Dyson." She stood and accepted his shake. "Please call me Reggie. You'll meet with my partner, Tyson Graham, after we chat."

They took their seats and Reggie opened his file and nodded. "I'm glad your emergency was resolved and we're able to talk. Your skills are impressive, and out of the forty applicants, your background stood out." He pushed back from the table and crossed his ankle on his knee. "Tell me about the government projects you've worked on."

She went through her spiel. "One program was identifying which neighborhoods had the highest number of high school dropout rates. We analyzed demographics and we were able to advise social agencies which services would benefit residents in certain zip codes."

Reggie was engaging as he scribbled notes. "When Tyson and I founded this company, we followed the money trail. Static billboards and now digital ones are money-makers. Referrals from ad agency was the major source of our revenue. We recently decided to shake things up and compete directly for clients instead of waiting for agencies to send business our way. Plus, we're part of the St. Louis minority council, so we're getting more business than we can handle, including some national conventions."

Monica's heart pounded with excitement. She wanted to be part of a growing company; working with a minority entrepreneur was a bonus. Yes, she wanted this job. "Since I heard about the opening, I've been paying attention to the ads on buses and other public transportation," she said.

"Great." Reggie bobbed his head. "But we are selective in accepting ads. We won't put liquor store or pawn shop ads on our billboards near the black communities."

Integrity. She respected a man willing to lose money because of his conviction.

Patting the tabletop, Reggie stood. "Miss Wyatt, I think you're a winner. I'll get Ty so you can chat with him a few minutes."

Once the man closed the door, she did a happy dance in her seat. *Yes!* One down and one to go. She would have to treat Solae to lunch when she received her first paycheck. The doorknob rattled and Monica snapped back into business mode and readied her smile.

The tall, dark, and more handsome man who entered could definitely be her crush. His black silky eyebrows and mustache—the best asset—seemed familiar, and those expressive dark eyes confirmed where they had met. This was the same man who came to her aid on the highway. When he gave her a look like a deer caught in headlights, she knew he recognized her too. She swallowed and watched him. Now what? If he didn't bring up the incident, she would play along and not say a word.

"Miss Wyatt," he greeted in a no-nonsense voice that was husky, an attention grabber, and a hypnotizer. "I'm Tyson Graham."

Take a deep breath, and don't groan! she chided herself.

His left hand—bare of a wedding band— flattened his stylish tie against his buff chest. Instead of taking the adjacent chair Reggie had vacated, he took a seat across from her, drawing an imaginary line between them. Where his partner came off as friendly and engaging, her first—second— impression of Tyson was less than favorable. He spoke with confidence, but his body language said otherwise. This was definitely awkward.

She'd seen concern in his brown eyes outside her car window. From the few glances he spared her, concern was there again. Opening his file to reveal her résumé, she watched as Tyson circled her name once, twice, three times.

He reminded her of a distracted student doodling on their paper when the teacher wasn't paying attention. Her résumé was a page and a half. Surely he had read it before today? He was stalling.

She resisted the urge to drum her fingers on the table, so she glanced at the flat screen. The sound was on mute, but the words crawling across the bottom might have been sending her a message: *signs to recognize when your life is in trouble.*

"Monica Wyatt." He cleared his voice and tapped his pen on the table.

Blinking from the screen, she faced him again and smiled. "Yes."

"Your background is in the non-profit sector. What do you know about advertising?" His tone held skepticism and he gave her a pointed stare as if he were seeing right through her.

Straightening in her chair, she chose her words carefully. Unlike Reggie, it seemed Tyson was going to make her fight for the position. "Numbers don't lie. Whether it's social services or products, if the data is analyzed correctly, a person will make the right choices based on demographics."

He nodded. Once he focused on her résumé again, she studied him. Tyson was well-groomed from his fingernails to the precision lining of his haircut. His lashes were jet black and so thick, they reminded her of the fake lash kit she had Veronica apply to hers unsuccessfully.

He closed the file and gave her a blank expression. "Why should we hire you, Miss Wyatt?"

"I'm very detail-oriented, I meet deadlines, and I—" She paused when he shook his head.

"On paper, you may be a perfect fit, but I'm referring to personality-wise. Deadlines can be stressful. How would you handle them?"

Was this a trick question? She dared not ask. Monica needed a job, no, she wanted this one. The competitive salary and benefits package was like getting a big raise from her last position and signing bonus. Still, she could do without his innuendos. If he had something to say, he should say it. Scratch that. Having no clue how to explain her actions, she played the game. "I'm a calm person by nature. Plus, I have a history of getting along with my peers. My references will agree."

"Very well." He gathered the file, stood, and twisted his lips as if he was debating something.

Monica wanted to scream, "Share."

He didn't. "You'll hear from us by the end of the week regarding our decision. Thanks for coming in today." By walking out of the room, had Tyson just shut her door of opportunity?

The sinking feeling in her chest caused her to blink back the moisture filling her eyes. *God, was this just a tease?*

How did she go from "you basically have the job" to "not sure you're a good fit" status? She could hear her mother chiding her with the old adage, "Don't count your eggs until they're hatched."

Ollie Wyatt might have been on point this time. The job had been a long shot anyway with her no-show earlier, but she had given the interview her best shot. Her legs wobbled as she got to her feet and it had nothing to do with her high heels. It was a good thing she hadn't told her mother about this interview. Her mother was a crier—happy or sad tears. No doubt, she would be *boo-hoo*ing alongside Monica about now.

But she got her fierceness from her dad and brother. She would hold her tears and strut out of the room as if the job didn't matter as much as it did. Her dignity would remain intact until she drove out of the parking lot. After taking a series of deep breaths, Monica opened the door. She could sense being watched, but she refused to scope out the interloper. Locking her eyes on the route to the double-glass doors in the lobby, she began her catwalk.

She was within feet of her escape when Solae almost bumped into her while looking at her smartphone. "Oh, I'm sorr—" She looked up. "How did the interview go?"

Overcome with emotion, she didn't want to voice her disappointment. Swallowing back tears, she struggled to say something. "I believe I won over Reggie, but didn't impress Mr. Graham."

Solae frowned. "Odd. Those two are usually on the same wavelength."

"Not today." Judging from Tyson's vibes, Monica had

better come up with a Plan B before her next car payment was due. "Thanks for referring me." Her voice cracked and she hurried out the door.

Chapter Three

The image of the fear in Monica Wyatt's brown eyes had haunted Tyson all weekend. More than once, he wondered if she was okay. Today, he had his answer. She was alive, acting well, and not going to work for his company—period.

He stuck his head into Reggie's office to give his decision, but his partner was on a call. The goofy expression on his face was the giveaway he was probably speaking with his girlfriend who he met months earlier while on a business trip. *Come on, man. Let's run a business*, Tyson tried to send a telepathic message. It didn't work.

"Be with you in a sec," Reggie mouthed and motioned for him to shut the door.

This wasn't the time to get blindsided by womanly distractions. As close friends as they were, he suspected Reggie would choose Tracee over him.

Returning to his office, Tyson collapsed in his chair and grunted as if seeing her again was funny. What were the odds the leading candidate for a job in his company and the polished beauty with the seductive brown eyes, full lips, and intoxicating perfume was the same dazed out woman on the highway?

Reggie, singing her praises minutes before Tyson walked into the room, had set him up for the biggest letdown. He had planned to co-sign his partner's decision. He was wowed by her beauty before recognition struck, then all he wanted to do was ask, "What happened? Are you okay? Why are you here?" Of course, her answers wouldn't have mattered. Tyson had seen enough in one instance to make a judgment call not to hire her. Her unstable behavior could be a liability. Now, he had to convince Reggie.

There were certain things Tyson would defend too rigorously—his family, his baby, and his heart. Since his parents and sisters were holding their own, that left his baby—Tyson & Dyson Communications.

Something told him Monica would not only challenge his head, but his heart as well. Somewhere deep inside of him was an urge to protect her—a stranger, and the impulse was so miniscule a pair of tweezers couldn't extract it.

In corporate America, Tyson had faced many challenges as a black man, being passed over for promotions and unwelcomed sexual advances, even by a supervisor, but his family jewels and things to do with his performance in the bedroom were not to be coerced. Unlike Reggie, Tyson knew how to separate business commitments from personal pleasure.

"Enough self-reflection," he mumbled and reached for a folder on the small stack of other applicants' résumés. Their credentials weren't as impressive as Monica's, but second best would have to do. He and Reggie had to get someone in there fast.

A knock on the door signaled it was time for Tyson to convince Reggie to trust his decision on this one. Instead, Solae slowly opened it. "You got a minute?"

Pushing the paperwork aside, Tyson nodded and folded his hands. "Yep, what you need?"

She frowned and stepped farther into his office. "What happened with Monica? She left here with the impression she didn't get the job? I thought she was about to cry."

Solae looked as if she was about to cry too. He gritted his teeth when he saw Reggie standing in the doorway.

The goofy expression was gone, replaced by a suspicious frown. "Yeah, what happened? I thought we had agreed she was exactly who we needed. The interview was a formality."

"Can you give Reggie and me a minute?" he asked Solae, who didn't appear happy about being excluded from the conversation, but she complied and gave them privacy.

Reggie took a seat and folded his arms. "Talk."

"I don't think she is a good fit. I'm not sure her non-profit background would transfer well into private sector."

"Uh-huh." Reggie shook his head. "That jargon isn't going to work on me, man. What's the real deal?"

Suddenly, he was having second thoughts as if he was about to betray her trust, which was ridiculous. He owed her nothing.

"What?" Reggie repeated.

"Ah," he stuttered. "There's something about her that makes me wonder if she's mentally stable."

Reggie threw his head back and laughed. "Really? She seemed stable to me when I talked to her. If left up to you, we would have an all-male workforce. You really need to work on your trust issues with women. Every chick doesn't have an agenda like the women from your past. Tracee has some friends." He smirked and nodded. "Yeah, definitely worth checking out and available."

Flabbergasted, Tyson leaned across his desk. "Reg, focus, man. I don't have time to think about a woman."

Liar. That's all you've been doing since you saw Monica, a voice taunted him.

Annoyed with his inner conscience, Tyson exhaled. "Listen, I didn't get a good feeling about—"

"Too bad." Reggie slapped his hands on his knees and got to his feet. "You know she'll make a great addition. I think we'd regret not hiring her for her expertise. Plus, Solae said they were practically family."

"Huh?" Tyson groaned. Did he have to be concerned about Solae having a meltdown too now? "She didn't mention that."

"Something about her family tree. Wyatt-Palmer was her maiden name. Anyway, unless you have something concrete, not suspicions, I suggest bringing her in on the three months' probation."

Speak now, or forever hold your peace, his mind said. Tyson opened his mouth to come clean about what he saw on the highway, but his tongue locked in position. Aggravated with his internal fighting, he conceded. "Three months. That's all Monica Wyatt has. You contact her." Reggie was almost out the door when Tyson added, "Oh, and make sure she gets the ten-panel drug test screening." The standard pre-employment drug test would only catch street drugs. He wanted to know of any prescription drugs misuse.

Rubbing his forehead, Tyson frowned. Unless the highway episode was a one-time occurrence, and he suspected it wasn't, it would be a matter of time before the other Miss Wyatt would show up again. And Reggie would see with his own eyes what Tyson failed to tell him.

"I didn't want the position anyway," Monica stated, as she checked on her beef stew simmering in the Crock-Pot.

"You're such a liar." Veronica *hmph*ed, then bumped her out of the way to wash her hands in the kitchen sink. Her friend had stopped by under the guise of getting details on what happened when she really came for the food.

Their friendship was based on Monica's cooking skills and Veronica's decorating genes. Friends since grade school, they were closer than sisters and each other's confidant. Veronica knew things Monica dared not share with her mother—the worrywart.

Besides getting a job, her mother had started hounding

her about grandbabies. In order for that to happen, she wanted more than a donor, she desired a man who loved her first and his family second.

She and Veronica were single and not satisfied. That's why they had added double dating on their New Year's resolutions list. Actually, it was nothing more than a ruse for her friend who could be engaged or married with children by now if she and Monica's brother's hearts ever aligned with the planets.

"Well, I hope I'm a good one, because my brain is starting to hurt every time I think about being in the same room with Tyson Graham." She spat out his name as if she had tasted expired milk. "It's a wonder seeing him didn't ignite a full-blown anxiety attack, because that man creeped me out." She shivered.

Veronica twisted her lips as she removed bowls from Monica's cabinet. "Ah, the tale of two strangers. I can't believe a man—in your words, handsome—so caring to stop and help a stranded motorist would be so cold. Maybe he was having a bad day."

"Believe me, I can understand having a bad day, but not on the day of my interview." She pulled rolls out of the oven as her cell rang. "Can you get that?"

"It's an unknown number," Veronica said, then answered. "One moment please." She handed Monica her phone and mouthed, "I should be having dinner with him." She grinned. "He sounds hot!"

Rolling her eyes, she snatched the phone. "This is Monica." She held her breath as the caller identified himself as Reggie Dyson.

"If you're still interested, we would like to offer you the position."

Monica's heart dropped, and so did her mouth. She was speechless; after grabbing the nearest chair, she floated down. "I got the job," she mouthed to Veronica.

Her friend began to dance around the kitchen with an

invisible partner. She froze and squinted. "Take it!" she threatened in a low sweet soft voice.

Reggie was in her corner. Was Tyson playing hardball with her, or did he cast a no vote? While Monica debated the unknown, Veronica grabbed a piece of discarded aluminum foil, bunched it into a ball, and bounced it off Monica's head.

She gave Veronica a "what's wrong with you?" scowl.

"Take it."

Closing her eyes, Monica took a deep breath. "I accept your offer," she said, then exhaled, thanked him, and ended the call. "I start on Wednesday"—she stood and pointed her finger— "and you're paying for the foil."

"Nope." Veronica lifted the lid to the Crock-Pot and inhaled. "Now that you're gainfully employed, you can afford to buy your own." Reaching for her bowl, she scooped up a hearty portion, grabbed a roll, and sat at the table.

Monica joined her with her own serving. She whispered a quick prayer, and added a thanks for the job.

"Since you'll no longer be stressed out about finding a job, your panic attacks are probably over."

"You're probably right." After high-fiving with Veronica, Monica ate without a care in the world.

Chapter Four

Two days later, Monica awoke with a feeling of doom. Considering what she read about her symptoms on the Internet, she was experiencing nothing more than morning anxiety.

The good news was the feeling of dread would dissipate as the day went on. After giving herself a pep talk while she dressed, Monica's confidence had bounced back by the time she headed out the door to her first day on the job.

Less than thirty minutes later, she drove into the company lot and parked. Making eye contact with the rear view mirror, she checked her makeup. She patted perspiration off her forehead and stared at her reflection. "Let's do it." She stepped out of her car with her briefcase and purse. She took a few minutes to study the building where she would spend her days until she decided to work elsewhere, if the time ever came.

Pleased with how everything turned out, she walked with a purpose through the front doors.

"Welcome back, dear, and congratulations," the same receptionist greeted her in the lobby. "I'm Maggie, but everyone calls me Mrs. Coates."

Seconds later, the door opened behind her and a cold

blast propelled Solae inside. "Hey, I tried to beat you here so I could show you around." She seemed out of breath.

"Our office has seven rooms," Mrs. Coates said, planting a fist on her hip. "I doubt she'll get lost."

Solae chuckled. "Come on, I'll take you to your corner office."

"Great." Monica wanted to dance in place. She was so excited to have an office again. Besides saying grace and a quick prayer when in distress, she wouldn't call herself a praying woman, but at the moment, she thanked God for putting Solae in her path.

If you call on Me, I will answer, a voice whispered.

Her steps slowed. That wasn't her imagination or conscience. She definitely heard a voice. Turning around, Monica saw no one; even Mrs. Coates had disappeared.

On the left, they passed two closed doors. "Across from Reggie and Tyson's offices is the conference room where you had your interview." Solae walked and talked.

They turned the corner to a large room with four spacious cubicles. "You're the last one in the back."

Monica grinned at her "corner office." She had the best view to a small park nearby. After waiting for Monica to store her things, Solae introduced her to the small staff: another designer, a copywriter, and an intern. The most interesting room was the kitchen with one side reminding her of an ice cream parlor.

Retracing their steps to the hall, Solae stopped at the first door and knocked before opening it. Reggie stood from his desk and extended his hand, walking toward her. "Mr. Dyson—"

"Please call me Reggie. We're informal around here."

"Okay." She smiled. "Thank you for the opportunity."

"Thanks for accepting. We're excited about adding your expertise in growing our company." Leaning on the corner of his desk, he folded his arms and chatted a few minutes.

When Solae backed out of the room and knocked on

door number two, Monica's heart pounded. She wouldn't consider seeing Tyson again as saving the best for last, but she was ready to dismiss their first impressions and start over.

Hiding behind Solae wasn't an option when the woman stepped aside and Monica came face-to-face with him.

Where Reggie stood immediately to greet her, Tyson hadn't even shifted in his seat as he removed his reading glasses. He seemed intimidating, serious, and almost annoyed at the interruption. Monica refused to let her disappointment show. The decision to hire her must have been all Reggie's. Well, she was there now and wasn't going anywhere. By default, he had seen her vulnerable side. Beginning today, she would show him her backbone.

Ignoring his display of bad manners, Monica showed him a smile she didn't feel. "Thank you, Mr. Graham, for the opportunity."

"You're welcome, Miss Wyatt." Evidently, he didn't feel like smiling.

The silence was becoming uncomfortable when finally, as if he remembered his home training, Tyson stood. If wearing black made a woman appear thin, it did the opposite for Tyson, who was dressed in a black shirt, pants, and another eye-catching tie. With each step toward her, she tried not to shrink under his imposing stature and build.

He seemed to begrudgingly extend his hand, then swallowed up hers. It was strong, yet gentle, and his cologne begged her to take a deep breath. Their point of contact caused a chill down her spine. She refused to succumb to whatever effect he was trying to have on her.

Lifting her chin in defiance was a mistake. Close up, she was drawn deeper into his hypnotic eyes. She saw uncertainty in them, or maybe it was a reflection of what he saw in hers.

Solae cleared her throat, breaking the frozen moment between her and Tyson. "Ah, Mrs. Coates has forms for you to sign. I'll go get them."

On cue, he released her hand and stepped back. If only

she knew what he was thinking? If—another if only—they had met under different circumstances, she could see herself being attracted to him.

Gnawing on her lips, Monica wondered if mentioning what happened would clear the air or make matters worse.

Don't you dare! She could hear Veronica's wise council.

"How was your weekend?" Tyson's question seemed forced.

Not one to engage in small talk, she didn't answer right away, considering it was Wednesday and she had to think what she did—nothing. "Nice."

Tyson stuffed his hands in his pants pockets. Although he said nothing more, he didn't take his eyes off her.

"Got them," Solae said, reappearing and waving forms in the air. "See you later, Ty."

Thankful to escape his presence, Monica didn't exhale until she reached her desk. Once she signed her w-2 and other paperwork, she scanned through the company's brag book. She was surprised and proud Tyson & Dyson Communications had been the agency behind some recognizable billboards. It appeared the company had some impressive leads. She began to study the numbers to interpret the demographics for the marketing campaign her bosses would present to a client. Reggie said the best training was to dig in, and he wasn't exaggerating.

Monica had been soaking in information until Solae announced lunch. As they ate in the "parlor," Solae chatted away, "My husband is a fire captain and sometimes he's gone days at a time, so I'm here on Mondays, Wednesdays, and Fridays. I'm a full-time mommy the other two days."

To Monica, Solae had it all—a husband and children. She admired any woman who somehow had beaten the odds to snag a loving family man.

"I don't have any sisters," Solae said, keeping Monica's mind from drifting again. "But my best friend, Candace, married my hubby's brother."

"I don't have any sisters either. My best friend, Veronica, dated my brother off and on for what seems like forever. He's finishing up his tour in the Middle East."

"Girl, we are too much alike. If we're not blood-related, we could always be sisters in Christ, if you ever decide to come back to church. No pressure." She smiled and Monica believed her.

After lunch, she sat with Solae and Dennis, the other ad designer, and watched them create some mock campaigns for existing clients. At times, they asked for her input. Monica saw why her position was so important. Location was everything. A billboard ad for million-dollar homes would be pointless in a depressed neighborhood.

The afternoon sped by and soon everyone said their good nights. As if her mother had a tracker, she called before Monica dropped her keys on the counter. Ollie was so predictable. "I thought I was supposed to call you?" That had been the consensus from their chat the previous evening.

"It's about time you caught a break," her mother said when Monica gave her the good news about the job. *"Your dad and I've been praying for you. We thought you might have to give up the condo and move back home. Do you need me to spend the night and help you pick out something to wear for your first day or do your hair?"* Her mother had been giddy with excitement.

"Mom, I'm good. This isn't my first job. It's just a new one. I know what to wear and how to style my natural hair. I'll call you and tell you all about my first day."

"Okay, I'll be waiting by the phone." After exchanging *"I love you's,"* they ended the call.

"I knew you would take too long, so how did it go?"

"Typical first day, trying to learn the job." She described the building, her "corner cubicle office" and her coworkers. There was no need to mention Tyson and his peculiar behavior, which had to be a result of him witnessing her under distress, something she dared not mention to her mom anyway and cause her to worry. As a stats expert, she ran the numbers in her head. Remove the stress from not paying bills from the equation and the odds were in her favor. "Mom, I'm tired and hungry, so I'm going to go so I can cook dinner."

Minutes later, Monica had barely changed out of her clothes when her doorbell rang, and Veronica was on her doorsteps. She walked in, removing her coat with each step. "What's the scoop?" She sniffed. "And what ya cookin'?"

"Spaghetti, if you and my mom let me. At work, a little weird. I only came in contact with Mr. Graham once when he handed me a proposal for a small black-owned hair supply chain that wants to expand into the St. Louis area." She took a package of hamburger out of the refrigerator, opened it, and began to season it. "Make yourself useful. Boil some water for the spaghetti."

She thought about Tyson. "He wasn't mean to me, but the few times we passed each other in the hall, it was like" — she paused, trying to find the right words to describe their brief encounters— "feeling he knows something about me and he's dangling it over my head—blackmail."

"Girl, forget him."

"If you saw him, you would see why that would be a hard task to accomplish." That's like telling a child not to watch cartoons and as soon as the mother's back is turned, the child sneaks a peek.

Chapter Five

Tyson had survived three days with Monica on his payroll, mainly by avoiding her except when absolutely necessary. Her soulful eyes would bring a man to his knees, which was why he restrained his glimpses into hers during the interview.

That morning, he caught a flash of her speed walking past his office. It wasn't fast enough for him not to notice her shapely legs in ankle boots. Suddenly, red was his favorite color of the day inspired by Monica's dress. The moment had served as a subliminal flirt, but he refused to take the bait and go after her for some idle conversation.

This was his workplace and he wasn't about to jeopardize his own code of conduct. Attractive women always seemed to have an agenda, wanting something from him he wasn't willing to give—a ring, his money, or his heart. Monica was no exception. She wanted this job and for him to overlook her mental breakdown. He rubbed the back of his neck. That image was hard to forget.

He had to keep reminding himself Tyson & Dyson Communications had hired Monica for her brains, not beauty. She had impressed him with both. He hadn't expected a one-day turnaround on the black hair chain analysis he had requested from her by Friday morning. She handed it to him midday Thursday and his professional persona almost slipped. He thought about complimenting Monica on her hair, but he knew better than to let his tongue take control.

Tyson and Reggie reviewed the report. Reggie had verbally congratulated her on the depth of her initial findings based on demographics, including nearby salons, strip malls, and other stats to drive business to the client. Tyson felt obligated to compliment her as well. She made it difficult to act natural around her. He wished he didn't know her secret, but knowing was a reminder to stay on the sidelines.

It was unusual for him to stick around the office until five on Fridays, but he and Reggie were determined to win the bid on the black hair chain. When he opened his door, Solae and Monica had their hats and coats on and were coming his way.

He waved. "Have a good weekend, Solae and Miss Wyatt."

As he turned the corner, he heard Solae's hushed voice. "I don't know what's going on with Tyson. He acts like he really doesn't like you."

"He doesn't," Monica replied.

That stung. Tyson cringed, but kept stepping as if he hadn't heard their whispers. Otherwise he would have turned around and corrected Monica. Liked her? What man wouldn't find her attractive? Plus, as an employee, she did superb work. He didn't trust her working for him. The loophole was if she displayed any signs of instability during her probationary period, he wouldn't be liable for recourse by terminating her.

On Saturday, the sting was still lingering in his head when he visited his parents. It bothered him to be labeled as the bad guy.

"One thing I can't stand is a moody man," Earline Graham fussed, wagging a serving ladle at him. How could Tyson zone out at the dinner table in front of his mother and sisters?

"Yeah, what's going on with you, bro?" Kim, his oldest sister, chimed in.

Tyson hunched over his second bowl of chili and cleared his throat. He carefully chose his words. "This woman—"

"Ha." His mother slapped the table. "That's all I needed to know." She grinned. Although her long hair was completely gray, her smile always cast a youthful glow on her face. "I'm finally getting me a daughter-in—"

"Hold it right there, Momma." He held up his hand. "There will never be a love connection between me and the crazy woman. I don't trust her." Tyson scowled and reached for his can of soda.

"Crazy? What did this chick do? Slit your tires, tried to burn down your house, or send harassing texts? Do Gail and I need to have a chat with Miss Crazy Lady about our brother?"

As the only son, his older and younger sisters seemed to think he needed protection instead of the other way around. Countless times, the pair had instilled fear into a female who was interested in him and Tyson didn't return the sentiment.

"Nothing like that. I think she has some mental condition going on. Her drug tests came back normal, but this woman isn't. One minute she's okay, but I've seen a different side of her."

Earline squinted. "Start from the beginning and don't leave anything out."

So Tyson confessed the burden he was carrying.

"If she's a threat to your company, why did you hire her?" Kim asked.

"Reggie did." He twisted his lips. "I could've fought harder, but Miss Wyatt's assets were impressive on paper, and frankly, she was the best candidate."

Gail, his baby sister, who had quietly listened, raised her hand as if she was sitting in one of Kim's classes. "As usual, you're overthinking this. Just because she was scared doesn't mean she's crazy. I'm scared of barking dogs. Something spooked her and evidently, you haven't made her comfortable to share those fears with you," she reasoned with him. "Poor Miss Wyatt. How old is she?"

"Thirty-one." When his mother and sisters exchanged glances, then grinned, he asked, "What?"

Clearing her throat, Kim took on a serious tone. "Does this Miss Wyatt look scary?"

"It depends," he answered. On the highway, definitely. At the office, anything but. Monica had plenty of hair in its natural state. He wondered how long it would be if the curls were straightened out. She had nice legs and an enticing shape. She was the complete package.

Kim tapped the table. "I'm exposed to some form of mental illness in children frequently. If they don't get help, it will manifest itself when they become adults. Maybe she went through some trauma," she said softly. "I read somewhere one in twenty-five or -six people deal with mental illness in a given year. Chalk up what you witnessed as Miss Wyatt's year."

"For some reason, you were meant to meet on that road before she came in for the interview, son." His mother nodded with a worried expression. "There are no coincidences with God, and speaking of the Lord. It's been a while since you came to church."

Oh no, she wasn't about to ambush him. Pushing back from the table, Tyson had to get away from the Graham women's scrutiny. "The chili was good, Momma. I'm stuffed." He patted his stomach and excused himself to the living room where his father was watching a game.

"Hey, Pops." He sat on the sofa and stretched out his arms. Why did rescuing a damsel in distress have to come with baggage? He focused on the flat screen until his mind synced with his eyes to follow the game.

"I heard your mother and sisters in there give you a hard time." Craig Graham chuckled without taking his eyes off the television. "My advice is to guard your heart and business. Women have hormones I still can't understand after all these years."

Hormones? Tyson had two sisters. He didn't even want to recall their meltdowns as teenagers.

On Monday morning, Tyson was about to enter his office when Solae blocked his path.

"Can we talk in private?" She invited herself in. "Monica told me what happened between you two."

"I see." Tyson laid his briefcase on the floor and removed his coat. Solae scooted a chair closer to his desk and flopped in it. He leaned on its corner and folded his arms. "And?"

"What she described isn't normal behavior." Tyson knew that, but he wanted to hear Solae's take. "Do you know what I think she needs?"

"Medication," he stated.

"Maybe," she said with a touch of pleading in her voice and disappointment draped on her face. "Is that why you acted like a bully around her?" Solae lifted her chin in defiance, daring him to deny it, which he did.

"I'm the one who is scared of the chick," he defended.

"You're six feet something and she's five feet something else, and you're terrified of her?"

"For the record, I'm six feet four and she's about five feet five without heels." He had summed up his calculation when they shook hands. "I'm concerned about her brain not functioning at a hundred percent. If her data analysis is off, we could miscalculate a campaign."

"Instead of being scared of her, you need to be concerned and pray for her." She folded her hands in demonstration as if he had never asked God for anything. His company was built on his mother's prayers and a loan from his dad, which he had just finished paying back.

"Hershel and I have been inviting you to church for a while and you always have an excuse. Now you have a reason. Monica—your employee—needs praying people around her. This is serious. God can heal her. It wasn't an accident she came to my church, or you met her on the side of the highway. Her condition is no accident."

"You lost me on the last part. Monica told you it's hereditary?" As a matter of fact, Solae had gone into very little detail about what was said.

Solae smirked as she got to her feet. "Service starts at eleven."

"Uh-uh." Tyson shook his head. "Stop right there. Do you realize Sunday is the Super Bowl? I'll say a prayer for her before and after the game."

"Men, *hmph*. I hope the rapture doesn't come while you're waiting for a touchdown, because you'll miss it. I'm holding you to pray for her." She gave him a game face, then left his office.

Tyson took his seat and spun around to look outside his window. He frowned, thinking on Solae's request. He prayed as much as the next person, but somehow his employee felt that was what Monica needed from him. An odd request, but one he would fulfill from his spot in front of the television.

A knock interrupted his musings. Twirling around, he found Mrs. Coates peeping her head inside. "Yes?"

"Mornin'. Fresh fruit and bagels just arrived." She was about to back out then stopped. "By the way, I like Monica. She's sharp."

Did someone mastermind a Join #TeamMonica billboard? Did everyone know what was going on with her besides him?

His intercom buzzed. "Ty, the webinar is about to start. Your office or mine?" Reggie asked.

"I'll be there in a sec." He was glad to talk business instead of hearing others' opinions about Monica. While making a beeline to the kitchen for juice and bagels, she was heading his way.

"Good morning, Mr. Graham," she stated with little eye contact and continued strutting. He watched her disappear into the ladies' room. Yeah, he had work to do. Mr. Graham was his father, who had thirty years on his thirty-six. Even his business associates called him Ty. She was a project he would begin to work on later.

Once he was situated at the round table in Reggie's office, they chatted about possibilities for the black hair chain. "I think Mr. Freeman's concept of buying in bulk is going to set him apart from his competition," Tyson said. "I didn't realize Koreans owned more than sixty percent of the market."

Reggie nodded. "I know. Based on the numbers Monica crunched, the black hair care market is almost a seven hundred million-dollar industry."

"I think we need to bring Solae, Mrs. Coates, and Monica in on the campaign," Tyson suggested.

Reggie wore a lopsided grin. "I'm glad you're warming up to Monica, because the sister is fine and single."

Not Monica again. Tyson put on his poker face. He was well aware of her physical assets, but along with them came the mental madness, for lack of a better term to describe it. "And you've got a girlfriend in Florida." He lifted an eyebrow. "Or has the long-distance relationship ran its mileage?"

"Nope. Tracee and I are solid as ever. Just lookin' out for my bro."

"You should know I don't mix business with pleasure," Tyson reminded him.

"Maybe if you had more pleasure in your life, you wouldn't be so uptight." Reggie stopped and snapped into business mode when the two presenters logged on to discuss strategies for out-of-home advertising to reach the seventy-plus percent of consumers who are away from home in the day time.

During the hour-plus webinar, he and Reggie made notes and emailed the presenters questions about new trends. People were taking notice of ads with personal messages paid for by family and small groups: tributes to a soldier killed in active duty, or requests for donations to an agency in the name of a child who died of cancer.

Afterward, Tyson stood and stretched. "That info couldn't have come at a better time with the launch of the black hair care campaign underway."

Reggie agreed. "We could include testimonials of before and after using their hair products. We can put Dennis and Solae to work on a mockup."

Walking out of Reggie's office, Tyson heard a burst of laughter. It could've only come from Monica's lips. He chuckled at the genuine sound of amusement. He wondered at what triggered the uncontrollable bark. He stepped closer to the kitchen and hid in the shadows. When his cover was blown, he strolled in under the guise of getting a bottled water, but not before catching a glimpse of a smile on Monica's face.

"Hey," Solae and Mrs. Coates said in unison. Monica didn't acknowledge him.

"Hey back, Monica, Solae, and Mrs. Coates. Enjoy your lunch." Their laughter ceased as he strolled out the room. Without a backward glance, he could feel eyes on him, because they were all too quiet. Tyson hoped one pair was Monica's.

Chapter Six

Monica sensed Tyson's presence before she spotted him in her peripheral vision.

"Tyson acts like he doesn't like you." Solae had stated the obvious as they headed to their cars last Friday.

"He doesn't. I made a bad first impression." And she explained.

"Did you two discuss this during the interview?"

"Nope." She shook her head. "He didn't mention it directly, but his body language hinted he remembered me and the incident and would hold it against me."

"The best solution is seeking the Lord. When we met at church, it wasn't by chance." Solae beamed. "God set you up for this job. Everything is going to be okay, because once the Lord speaks, even the demons tremble. To be blunt, it sounds like you're wrestling with dark spirits in high places. The fear you experienced comes from the devil."

Great. Monica didn't do scary movies or read suspense novels. "How am I to win a battle against an enemy I can't see?"

Solae responded with a prayer, "Lord, in the mighty name of Jesus, please shield Monica's mind and body from the devil's attacks."

Monica silently added an addendum: Lord, just take them away.

The prayer must have worked over the weekend, because today Monica felt rejuvenated and carefree. Her attitude was now one man would no longer intimidate her in the workplace.

Well, sort of. How long had Tyson been standing in the shadows outside the doorway as she, Solae, and Mrs. Coates watched a funny video on Facebook?

When he made his presence known and greeted them, his tone was gentler. Absent was the clipped inflection when he said Miss Wyatt. Briefly, his persona was a glimpse of the man who came to her rescue. She halted any kind of whimsical thinking. Memories of that dreaded day reminded her why there was an invisible line between them. Even though she best not forget that, Monica no longer felt caged.

Too bad he judged her based on that first encounter, because he was irresistible to behold, dressed well, smart, and his cologne was like a welcoming air freshener.

"Don't think we didn't notice he said your name," Solae said with a smug smile and the elderly woman winked in agreement.

As Mrs. Coates stood, she gathered her trash, humming the old Destiny's Child tune "Say My Name."

Solae gasped. "You know that song?"

"I ain't that old," she sassed over her shoulder, leaving them alone in the kitchen.

They burst out laughing until Solae's eyes watered and Monica's stomach ached.

Her work week ended drama-free. Plus, she received her first pay check in three months. In good spirits, Monica shut down her computer and reached for her purse when she felt a familiar presence again. Tyson was standing at her desk. "Do you have a minute?"

The softness in his rich voice could make a woman close her eyes and dream she was on a beach, the wind blowing through her hair, and the sun kissing her skin. However, she didn't feel the security of one of those moments. It was quitting time and her boss was at her desk. Was he about to fire her?

Take a deep breath and don't let him see you sweat. "You're the boss." Folding her hands, she braced herself.

"Can we call a truce?"

She blinked and remembered to exhale. Not only was she not expecting that, Monica was suspicious of it. Why all of a sudden? But who was she to challenge him? "Sure."

Watching him, she waited for his next move or statement. Did Tyson want to talk about the highway incident? Was he expecting her to bring it up? There were too many questions, and he didn't open his mouth to say more. Actually, he was making her nervous.

"Well." She stood and gathered her coat. He took it from her and helped her put it on. Monica thought she would faint from shock. "Thanks," she whispered to mask her shaking voice. On unsteady legs, she hurried past him, taking the scent of his cologne with her. "Ah, have a nice weekend."

"You too, Monica."

She smiled, liking his husky voice saying her name.

Tyson watched Monica go. His mother and everyone would be proud he had extended an olive branch, although it took him all week to come up with five words to form a sentence.

He had watched Monica with interest. She was intelligent, beautiful, and grew more vocal in her work every day. He actually admired her, but on the flip side, he found himself attracted to her too.

Rubbing the back of his neck, Tyson sighed as he walked back to his office. What was he going to do about it?

"Absolutely nothing," he mumbled, reaching for his coat. With his keys already in the car, he headed for his SUV. He had more pressing matters.

On Sunday, Tyson and other fellow sports junkies descended on Reggie's house to watch the Super Bowl. He hosted the event last year at his loft. This year, the chips fell on Reggie.

He had been hyped all weekend, waiting for his favorite

Sunday of the year. The addiction had been in his blood since high school, but Monica's soft features kept insinuating into his mind when he least expected followed by Solae's subtle reminder to pray for her.

And he did when he blessed his breakfast and even while dressing, which was a task, listening to the sports commentators on radio and television. Pulling for the Kansas City Chiefs, Tyson donned the team's jersey and cap before he left.

He parked in front of Reggie's West End home and smirked at the New England Patriots team flags anchored on the front and back windows of a black SUV. Another friend, Jimmy, had beat him there.

When it came to sport teams from the East Coast, Jimmy lost his mind.

As he climbed the steps to the front door, loud voices on the other side meant Jimmy had brought Patriots reinforcements. He didn't bother knocking and opened the door. He was jeered and cheered on by the guys as if he had entered a playing field. Getting caught up in the spirit, Tyson bobbed his head and gave them high fives, stepping his way down a Soul Train line. Yes, this was his type of party.

The last of the invitees arrived. Fred was another Patriots cohort who strolled through the door outfitted in gear as if the party was outside: skullcap, jacket, and—once it was removed—sweater, and gloves. If that wasn't insane enough, Fred opened a thermal lunch box to display his own Patriots eating paraphernalia: plastic tumbler, bowl, plate, and other unidentifiable items.

Tyson and Reggie had never laughed so hard.

Despite the chilly temperature and an inch of snow on the ground, Reggie had meat on the grill, their tradition, but a few times, through business connections, they hit the road after securing complimentary Super Bowl tickets.

But Reggie had compromised their male-bonding tradition this year. Of all the fifty-two weekends, Tracee

EVERY WOMAN NEEDS A PRAYING MAN

picked Super Bowl Sunday to visit. He and the others would do their best to be respectful. Otherwise, their host would put out every last man if they offended his lady.

Reggie had lost his mind over Tracee, no, he had freely handed his heart over to the woman. If she called, Reggie jumped with the excuse, "My woman needs me," or "she's missing me." How long would their long-distance relationship last? For Tyson, that wouldn't work. He would have to see his woman on a regular basis. Definitely more than a few times a month Reggie got to see Tracee, and that's if they could manage to get away.

Despite being a die-hard football fanatic, Tyson's attention strayed to the couple more times than he could count. In the midst of the trash-talking testosterones, Reggie and Tracee seemed to be in their own private place. Witnessing their harmony sparked a yearning in Tyson.

He hadn't dated seriously since the previous summer and the few casual dinners he shared had been less than memorable. The women had been pretty, professional and…hmmm. Tyson couldn't remember much more about them. Unlike Monica—Tyson held his breath. *Where did she come from?*

He shook the dust balls out of his head. He glued his eyes to the Chiefs' running back at the forty-yard line, then thirty, twenty, racing for the touchdown. Three Patriots were gaining speed until a flag was called on Kansas City for holding. "What!" Tyson balled his fists as Jimmy gave out fist bumps to his buddies.

Monica's game face resurfaced. He closed his eyes. Why in the middle of the most important game was she taunting him? She agreed to the truce, so why couldn't he dismiss her?

"Touchdown!" Patriots sympathizers shouted and leaped, singing, "We are the champions…"

Their antics slapped0 him back to reality. Tyson hadn't realized he had zoned out, missing the Patriots barely score a touchdown.

Maybe he should've attended church before the game's festivities to clear his head of all distractions, especially the pretty one with soulful eyes. She might not be there with him, but she had commandeered his pastime.

Chapter Seven

Although Monica wasn't into sports, she sat through the Super Bowl in Alexander's honor while he was deployed. Somehow, her father knew how to tune out her mother's chatter.

"You need to start thinking about getting married," Ollie wormed her agenda into the game every time a penalty was called.

Like I don't. Monica sighed. "Mom, I think most women dream about their wedding day from the time they're little girls, but I need a groom to pull it off. Currently, there are none in sight." Although she said it in a nonchalant manner, she would rather cook for a husband than Veronica. Yet, Monica held out hope her egg bank would hold her deposits at least for another decade.

"That's because my shotgun has scared them off," her father stated without taking his eyes off the screen.

She and her mother chuckled, but Monica knew the man who wanted to marry her would have to get George Wyatt's stamp of approval.

On Monday, the staff held a pow-wow in the conference and hashed out details for the black hair store chain campaign.

Monica had taken the lead, passing out her analysis sheets. "I identified ten minority neighborhoods that don't have a beauty supply store within walking distance, which means they drive for what they want. The billboards in the zip codes I highlighted in yellow would target those demographics."

When Reggie had congratulated her, Monica smiled; her mind played tricks on her and she blinked, after she imagined she saw a slight wink coming from Tyson. Men weren't generous with that gesture unless they were flirting. This was a business setting and since the truce, Tyson was the epitome of professionalism toward her. When she eyed him again, his attention was elsewhere. Had to be her imagination.

Solae took the floor next. "I'm envisioning adhering vinyl posters on the back of buses with an African American model with a head full of natural hair like Monica." She paused as everyone glanced her way. "The model could have an alluring smile with a curled finger—"

"Yes!" Dennis interrupted. His eyes were wide with excitement. "Add the caption: Follow Me to Freeman Brothers Beauty Supply." He turned and lifted his hand.

Solae gave him a high five.

"Sounds like a winner," Reggie said and they all agreed.

So for the entire week, everybody had been crazy busy trying to fine-tune the campaign. Monica tried not to think about the upcoming Valentine's Day, but on Friday, the day was hard to ignore when she arrived at work and flowers had hijacked the counter in the lobby.

Mrs. Coates popped up, grinning from ear to ear. "My kids and grandkids," she explained without Monica asking.

"Lucky you."

Continuing on to her workstation, Monica couldn't help but notice the large bouquet of red roses waiting on their intern's desk who had yet to arrive. Lucky Jennifer. Odd though, was Solae's work station where no flowers were in sight. Monica assumed her friend would probably get a delivery sometime today. Speaking on the phone, Solae waved.

Monica dared not have a pity party. It's not like she got flowers every Valentine's Day, but she had plans. She and Veronica would brave the lines at Crown Candy, the historic St. Louis eatery, and purchase a pound of white chocolate-covered strawberries. Later tonight, they would watch romantic movies and gorge out on carryout and their treats.

At her desk, Monica got to work. Her mind was caught up in the numbers when Solae peeked around her cubicle. "Break time. Mrs. Coates usually has Valentine's cookies or cupcakes delivered. C'mon, let's pig out."

While in the kitchen, sampling the treats, Monica saw their intern heading toward them, smiling and carrying a small balloon bouquet.

"From my boyfriend," Jennifer offered.

"I already sent my lady one." Reggie nodded, seemingly pleased with himself.

The other men mumbled dinner plans, but Monica didn't hear anything coming from Tyson as others filled out of the kitchen, leaving Monica and Solae to sample the treats.

"Mommie…Mommie."

She and Solae spun around to see a fireball running their way. Solae's daughter latched on to her legs. Two older boys trailed behind their sister. Each child carried a single rose. "Aww." Solae rewarded each one with loud kisses on their cheeks. The boys blushed. "Monica, you haven't met my sons. Harrison is six and Brandon, eight."

They were adorable now, but when maturity kicked in, they would be handsome like their father who watched nearby with sparkles in his eyes and a bouquet of roses in his hand.

Blinking away moisture, Monica fought back jealousy, not so much of Solae, but what her coworker had: a family of her own.

Okay, this is becoming overwhelming. Maybe Monica shouldn't have broken off her engagement with Daren last year. She could be a mother by now. Then again, her ex never gazed at her with so much love in his eyes. She turned to leave and give the family some privacy when Solae stopped her.

"I want you to meet my handsome husband, Hershel."

The man actually blushed and he extended his hand for a shake. "That's the way she always introduces me. I think I'm going to change it on my birth certificate."

Monica smiled and thought, *Why? Your wife is telling the truth.* "So Hershey is named after her father?" She noted the pride on Hershel's face as confirmation.

"Actually, her legal name is Madison, but I've been calling her Hershey since day one," Solae explained as her husband pulled her closer. "You'll meet more handsome hunks later this month at the Black Firefighters Ball, so get to shopping, girl."

"Babe, I've got to get the boys back to school. This was their idea to surprise their mother." He kissed her cheek to the boys' protests. Tyson and Reggie strolled by and stopped to greet Solae's husband, shaking his hand. Monica used their appearance to disappear to her private space. This Valentine's Day may turn out to be the most emotional yet.

At her desk, she reached for a tissue and dabbed her eyes, careful not to smear her makeup. "I've got the car and now the job. God, can I have what Solae has, too?"

No good thing will I withhold to those who love Me, was whispered in her ear.

Was that God talking to her? What did He mean? Monica felt she loved God as much as the next person, but while He let Solae enjoy a perfect life, what man would want a woman who would freak out at a moment's notice? Even God didn't have an answer.

Seeing the longing on Monica's face as she watched Solae and Hershel's exchange made Tyson's heart slam against his chest, dip to his stomach, and bounce back again. She tried to mask it when she hurried away, but he caught a glimpse of the sadness in her eyes. Suddenly, they were back on the highway and Tyson found himself in protective mode.

While conversing with Hershel, his mind was on Monica. If he didn't fight off these emotions she yanked in his heart, she would have him wrapped around his fingers. That was not good on so many fronts; for one, he didn't date in the workplace, and she had unresolved issues.

Tyson slipped back into his office and closed the door. He gritted his teeth and balled his fists. What was going on with him? He pounded his desk, wanting an immediate answer.

By the end of the day, it didn't go unnoticed Monica was the only female employee who didn't receive a floral delivery. Among the four male employees, Tyson was the sole one who didn't have a special someone. So by default, he and Monica were two peas in a pod.

Growing up, Tyson's father had taught him to give his mother candy and gifts, but the only man who would give Earline flowers would be her husband. Tyson smiled, remembering Craig Graham patting his chest during one of many of their father-and-son chats. "When you get a wife, always take her flowers."

Reggie stuck his head into Tyson's office, pulling him back into the present. "Heading to the airport." He waved.

"Earn those frequent flyer miles, bro. Tell Tracee hi. I haven't seen her in ages," Tyson joked.

"Hater." Reggie laughed and closed the door.

Maybe he was, but before Tyson left the office, he had one more thing to do. What was it about Monica that made him want to be her rescuer? Picking up the phone, he called a nearby florist.

Chapter Eight

Monday morning, Monica watched Mrs. Coates make a grand entrance into the kitchen. "Flowers for you," she sang.

"Me?" She patted her chest and squinted at the red roses blooming from a translucent vase. The contrasting colors had a wow factor. There was no one in the room except her, but still she repeated, "For me?"

The woman nodded. Her eyes twinkled with suspicion.

"Do you know who they're from?" Monica steadied her hand to rest her glass of water on the counter, then reached for the vase.

"Now, I would have to open the envelope to know that, and I'm too old to be in a federal prison for tampering with U.S. Mail."

Unless the flowers arrived through the mail, the woman was safe. Of course, Monica didn't want to give her any reason to be nosy.

"You've been holding back on us." Mrs. Coates giggled. "I was about to set you up with my grandson. He's good-looking—if I may say so myself—has a union job at a warehouse, and recently moved out of my daughter's house."

Recently moved out of his mother's house. "How old is he?" she asked out of curiosity, not interest.

"Turns thirty-seven in December. He was a Christmas baby," she boasted. "Well, you think about it. Kenny's never been married and doesn't have any children."

Right. Nothing to consider. Monica nodded and waited for the woman to leave. She ripped open the envelope in her effort to get to the card. *You're a Special Valentine.*

Aww. Her heart pounded, accepting the compliment. Turning the card over, she found no signature. Odd. "A secret admirer?" she mumbled. That hadn't happened since second grade.

Fingering the petals, she closed her eyes and leaned in to inhale the fragrance. As her lids fluttered open, she got lost in the vibrant color of red. Who sent them? Why not on Valentine's Day? She had no answers. Too bad Solae had taken Monday off, so she wasn't around to help her solve the puzzle.

Twirling around, Monica was startled to see Tyson standing in the doorway. The suspicious look he gave her made her feel like a kid caught stealing from the cookie jar. A smile tugged at the corners of his lips as he glanced from her to the flowers. "Nice."

He didn't have to know the sender was a mystery to her. "Somebody likes me," Monica said casually.

He lifted an eyebrow. "Indeed. He has good taste." With a smug expression, he walked away to answer a call on his cell.

After scooping up her vase, Monica almost glided to her desk. She had the perfect spot for them. At the moment, the sender didn't matter. The gesture made her feel cherished and not forgotten.

Whoever sent them had no idea they had made her day. She rearranged the vase three times until she was satisfied its location had a perfect view of the sun.

She called Veronica next. "Hey," she said in a hushed voice when her friend answered. "You're not going to believe this, but guess what I got?" She grinned.

"A raise!"

"Nope." Monica didn't have the patience to tell her to keep guessing. "Flowers!"

"Flowers? Who are they from?"

Spinning her chair around, Monica faced the window. "I have no idea who sent them. Maybe Daddy or Alexander. Right now, I don't care if they're from Mrs. Coates's grandson."

"Who?"

"Never mind."

"Well, all I know is your brother better not be sending flowers and not include me." She *hmph*ed.

"You two broke up again," Monica reminded her.

"Doesn't matter. Flowers are a girl's best friend."

Monica giggled. "Ah, I think that's diamonds."

"Starts with the flowers," Veronica said, then became quiet. "Seriously, you have no clue who sent them?"

Instead of answering, Monica closed her eyes and took a deep breath to enjoy the fragrance. "I may have to go home because I don't know if I can get any work done today." She rocked back in her chair. "Girl, they're gorgeous. Here, let me take a picture…" When she spun around, Tyson was standing there. She jumped. If she could slid under her desk, she would have. She didn't care if he'd heard she didn't know who sent them. Monica was concerned about the "she wasn't going to get any work done today" part.

"Hey, let me call you back." She ended the call and folded her hands. "Sorry, I didn't realize you were waiting for me. Yes?"

His brown eyes seemed to be dancing in merriment. What part was the source of his amusement? He was about to push her vase aside, but Monica shooed him away. "No! I'll move it."

He lifted his hands as if he was being held up. "I wanted to go over this client with you. Unless you plan to go home for some reason." He shrugged and snickered.

Monica scrunched her face. "You heard that?" Now

would be a good time to die of embarrassment and they could bury her with the roses. "Busted."

"Yes, you are." When he laughed, she released her signature bark that blended in with his. "We're good, but you can't go home. I have questions about the demographics on this." He waved a file in his hand.

Relieved and relaxed, Monica smiled as she moved her vase. It felt good to laugh with him. He waited while she tapped on her keyboard to bring up the spreadsheet.

The musky scent of Tyson's cologne arrested her senses when he peered over her shoulder at the screen. It was like a tranquilizer, slowing her movements.

Fighting the druggy feeling, she excused herself to the ladies' room. After using the facility, she washed her hands and stared at her reflection. What was going on with her? Her fingers felt numb and her heart raced. Was Tyson's closeness triggering a panic attack? Grinning, Monica shook her head. That wouldn't be a bad tradeoff from the other one.

Discussing a report with Monica had been a ruse. Curiosity drove him to her desk to see it decorated with flowers like Solae and Jennifer's.

Her blush had been priceless. Once he returned to his office, Tyson couldn't stop the grin from spreading across his face like a rash. He didn't mean to sneak up on Monica, but he had to know if the flowers had any effect on her. The stunt he pulled had cost him. Tyson Graham had crossed the line in employer and employee code of conduct and he had no idea how to keep himself from breaking the rules again.

Chapter Nine

A few days later, Monica couldn't believe she had lost track of time crunching the data for the State Education project. When she realized the sun was setting, she shut down her computer, grabbed her things, and left.

Inside her car, she shivered from the cold, so she started the engine to get the heat going. As she backed out, the hairs on her body tingled, alerting her of an impending sense of danger. The sensation wasn't overpowering, but a hint a panic attack was on the sidelines, waiting to pounce on her.

Monica wasn't under any kind of stress, so she ignored the tease. She took off to exit the parking lot when her hands began to shake and her breathing became labored. Maybe, this time, she was having a heart attack. "God, why me?"

Closing her eyes, she rested her head on the steering wheel and coaxed herself to calm down. She tried to remember the breathing exercises Veronica had advised, and praying as Solae had suggested. Although her mind jumbled, Monica managed, "God, please help me." She had to get home, even if it meant taking the back roads.

A tap on her window made her look up. It was déjà vu. Tyson was standing there with his intense stare. No, not again.

"Are you okay?"

She nodded, but not convincingly. She just wanted this moment to pass and for him to go away.

"Open the door, Monica," he ordered. With very little fight left in her, she complied.

"I can either give you a lift home in my SUV—"

She shook her head. "I'm good."

"That's debatable." Twisting his mouth, Tyson seemed annoyed. "I'm going to back up, so you can park your car."

"Huh?" Her brain was shutting down because she couldn't comprehend.

"I'm driving you home," he said softly. "I don't want you on the road like this."

No. This was a private meltdown. A website said an attack could last anywhere from ten to thirty minutes. How much time did she have left? While she was attempting her calculation, Tyson fumed.

"We can do this my way, which is to call the paramedics, or your way, which is still my way, and I drive you home."

Bully, she thought. But right now, she needed this bully to take control. "All right."

He backed up his SUV so she could make a U-turn in the lot and park. She turned off the ignition as her heart raced. She was a nervous wreck.

Tyson opened her door. Without protesting, she let him escort her to the passenger side. Behind her wheel, he adjusted the heat and seat to accommodate his long legs. "Nice car. What's your address?"

Tears were already blurring her vision from the humiliation. When Monica opened her mouth, the floodgate of emotions released and she began to ball. This wasn't her. He would fire her for sure. The thought made her cry harder.

"Hey, hey." Tyson's voice was soothing as one of his strong hands pried the fist of her hand open, then squeezed it gently. "I'm here. Everything's going to be okay. Do you need me to take you to the emergency room?"

"I can't. I don't have insurance yet." That set off another

crying binge. This was so pathetic. She hadn't cried this much in one day since her mother withheld her allowance as a teenager for lying about something she couldn't remember.

"Right." He was silent and didn't rush her, but waited.

She dared not open her eyes to see the pitiful expression he was probably casting her way.

Once she reined in her emotions, he asked for her address again. She obliged.

After he programmed the GPS on his phone, he took off for the highway. Although she wasn't driving, the potential mental torture seemed to be waiting for her. It never materialized as she glanced out the window. Despite the embarrassment, she was grateful he didn't try to engage her in idle conversation. She needed the quiet time to make sense of her actions.

Closing her eyes, she allowed her mind to drift. When the car stopped, she stirred. Her lids fluttered open and she sighed with relief, recognizing her condo.

"You're home, Sleeping Beauty."

She chanced a glance at him. "I wasn't asleep. Besides, I imagine I'm anything but a beauty right now."

"You're still beautiful," he assured her. "Come on, get your things."

He shut off her motor and walked beside her to her door—her safe haven.

Tyson didn't leave her at the doorsteps, instead he came inside. Monica was too drained to show hospitality. She didn't even bother hanging her coat or taking his. She needed alone time and the sooner he left, the better. Then realization dawned, in order for him to leave, she would have to drive him somewhere.

Leaving Tyson to glance around her condo, she disappeared into her bathroom and stared at her reflection. Remnants of horror lingered on her face. Add shame to the mix and Veronica would call her a hot mess. She patted cold water on her face to remove whatever makeup was left, wishing she could wash away the memory of what happened.

"Monica," Tyson called from the living room.

Instead of answering, she kicked off her shoes and padded back to the living room. He patted the space next to him on the sofa, watching her. She swallowed the lump in her throat and fumbled with her fingers as she opted for the farthest distance from him.

Breaking eye contact with her, he scooted to the edge and seemed to study her floor. "I have to admit I have no idea what happened in the parking lot to spook you," Tyson spoke softly. "What can I do to help?" He faced her again.

She searched his eyes and saw kindness, so she pleaded, "Don't fire me."

"Done."

She exhaled. "Thank you."

"When did this start happening?"

"This" —she waved her hands in the air— "started months ago...I had a lot of changes in my life. I got laid off and I broke it off with my fiancé."

"You were engaged?" Shock or disbelief crossed his face.

Monica bobbed her head. "I don't know why he asked and why I said yes. I didn't love him enough for a happy ever after. The breakup wasn't stressful, but the relationship was, because at thirty back then, I was willing to settle for a decent guy and Daren was that much." Did they have to talk about something that didn't matter?

Why did I ask her that? Unless he cared. Tyson had told Solae the truth, he was scared—not of Monica, but for her.

When he came out of the building, he was surprised to see her just leaving too. When she didn't take off, he got out to investigate. That daze in her eyes caused his adrenalin to kick into overdrive. The only thing he cared about was her safety.

So now, as he sat in her living room, he made up his mind not to go until he was sure she was okay. Then he figured out how to get his car: call a cab or Reggie. No way was Monica getting back on the road.

"I'll pay your medical bills. You've got to get help."

"I will in sixty-five days."

She had been counting? Tyson didn't know what to make of that. Shaking his head, he answered, "I'm not talking as your boss. Ever since I saw you on that highway until you walked into my company, a part of my heart wondered what happened to you. If you were okay?"

"Until you had to interview me," she stated the obvious and stood. "Keep your money; I don't want to be indebted to you."

He chuckled. "You know you work for me."

"Reggie signs the checks."

Was that fight in her coming back? He smirked. "Same thing…I can't begin to tell you how sorry I am for the way I treated you. I didn't know if you were strung out on drugs or what. I'm sorry I judged you."

"Thank you for saying that. I accept." She moved toward the kitchen. "Since I don't know how long you plan to stay, I might as well feed you. There's leftovers."

"My mother taught me never to turn down a home-cooked meal." Even though her condo had an open floor where the kitchen, family room, and dining were all connected, Tyson got to his feet and trailed her. Choosing a stool, he sat at the counter to be close to her. "It is home cooked, right? Not frozen," he joked and was rewarded with a mischievous smile. He liked how her full lips curled.

"As far as getting my car…" He whipped out his smartphone. "I can call Reggie for a—"

"No!" That panic look was back on her face. "Please…don't share this with him or anyone else at work. Take my car," she offered hastily. "I can have my girlfriend give me a ride in the morning."

"Or, I can pick you up in the morning. I believe we're going the same way."

She gnawed on her lips before agreeing.

Tyson was convinced now more than before she needed help, and somehow, he had to convince her not to wait. If he was a cat with nine lives, Monica took eight of them tonight.

In less than fifteen minutes, they were breaking bread over homemade chicken lasagna and seven-layer salad. They started off talking about work, but he kept steering the conversation back to her personal life.

Besides being blessed with a shapely figure, which included sculptured legs he hadn't seen enough of—he blamed the winter weather as the culprit—her best physical assets were those eyes. They could woo a man into a trance.

"I still don't understand. You have so much going for you. Why would you consider settling in a relationship?" He smacked his lips. "By the way, woman, you can cook!"

She blushed and his heart responded by turning somersaults. "Thank you. My best friend, Veronica, says our friendship is bound by my food." They laughed.

"But she and I have done an informal survey. Women who have…" she made quotation marks with her fingers, "…it going on, as you say, are being cast aside for women who have children, as if they're needed more, which I guess they are. I don't think a job, home, and car completes a person's life. I work to live my life, not live strictly to go to work every day."

She held up her hands. "I'm talking in general. I like working for you and Reggie. I wanted the big 'c' companionship, I was willing to accept the small 'c' and compromise."

He reached across the table and took her free hand. "Listen to me. Every poll has at least a four percent margin of error. You work with numbers. Your unofficial survey had a whopping ninety percent error. I—" he patted his chest, "—will take a confident woman any day because I could trust her with my heart. Don't compromise, Monica, if you can get whatever asking price for your worth."

PAT SIMMONS

When she blinked, he removed his hand and scooped up the last bite of pasta into his mouth. He was sharing more than he was gleaning. He wiped his mouth. "Well, it's getting late. I better go. Are you sure it's okay for me to take your car?"

She nodded and smiled.

"I'll go straight home and not joyride," Tyson taunted to earn another smile from her. "Seriously, are you okay? I won't leave until I know you feel safe." He peered deep into her eyes and searched for bread crumbs of fear—all clear.

"You made me feel safe," she said softly as she retrieved his coat from the sofa.

At her door, the strangest emotion came over him. He wanted to wrap her in his arms and kiss her good night. But he resisted the urge and left.

58

Chapter Ten

A nightmare invaded Monica's sweet dreams about Tyson, stirring her awake. Pulling the covers back, she got out of bed and peeped out the window. Her car was missing in the driveway. Either someone stole it, which would have been her preference, or she really did freak out last night and her boss had to drive her home.

Rubbing her face, she groaned again. Since she couldn't return to sleep, Monica started her day two hours earlier. Somewhat refreshed by a shower and a cup of coffee, she called Veronica and gave her a play-by-play of what had happened.

"Number one," she finally snapped, "you should have called me last night—"

"And deal with your wrath for disturbing your beauty rest? No thanks." Not a morning person, Veronica would sleep until noon every day, if she could, but she was well paid to report to work by seven. That translated to going to bed early. She walked into the bathroom to start on her makeup after slipping on her clothes.

"I'll ignore that…you and these attacks are aging me! I add wrinkles every time you tell me about them. At least you weren't alone, although I wish you had called, so I could've drove over to check out Mr. Graham." She chuckled and Monica shook her head, causing her to smear her eyebrow pencil. While she repaired it, Veronica continued her rant, "And third—"

"What happened to number two?" she teased.

"Be quiet. I can count. I'm not fully awake. Anyway, if the man offered to foot the bill, you should have accepted it like you won a cruise."

"And be a charity case? I can wait until my insurance kicks in." She hoped.

"Well, I can't, and if Miss Ollie knew…"

If her mother knew, she would move in with Monica uninvited. The doorbell rang. "Hey, that's my ride."

"Literally, call me the minute you get home this evening. Love you."

Yeah, this evening. She closed her eyes and whispered a prayer that she wouldn't have a repeat of the previous night. Why wasn't God listening to her? "Right. Love you too, sis. Bye."

She raced to answer the door, not wanting to be the cause—again—of her boss being late for work. When Monica opened it, Tyson's woozy cologne drifted inside. A fresh-shaven man was always her weakness. Their business relationship didn't give her liberties to touch his jaw.

"At your service." He smirked, activating a slight dimple that seemed to wink and go back into hiding.

"Let me get my coat and briefcase."

He stepped inside and closed the door. "Wait." He gave her an intense expression.

Twirling around, she asked, "Ah, is something wrong?"

Tilting his head, he seemed to study her. "Your skin is flawless. You don't have beauty marks."

She frowned. "Excuse me, was that a compliment or something?"

"An observation." Tyson snickered. "I didn't realize you have a tiny mole under your right eye. It's cute." He stuffed his hands in his coat pockets.

"What?" She studied her reflection in a nearby decorative mirror in her hall. She hadn't completely wiped off the smudge of her eye pencil, but it was barely visible, even she'd missed it. Yet, he had noticed it. What else had he observed about her?

"Little can distract from your beauty, trust me," he said in a casual manner, as if he didn't have to think about it.

Monica didn't want to read more into his statement, so she tried to clear her head. When she reached for her coat, he took it and helped her slip her arms inside as he had done at work. His closeness tickled the hairs on her neck, so she put some distance between them by hurrying to open her door.

"Feel up to driving this morning, or would you prefer my chauffeur services again?" He jiggled her car keys as they stepped outside.

The only nervousness she felt was being close to her boss.

Evidently, her hesitation caused him to touch her elbow and guide her to the passenger side. "I don't mind giving you curb service."

Once they were buckled up, he gave her a worried look. "Are you going to be able to drive back this evening?"

"Yep." She prayed that she wasn't lying.

Tyson hoped he hadn't embarrassed her, but every time he studied her, he saw something else alluring. She didn't have any marks, moles, or blemishes. He knew that for a fact. Her face had sweetly haunted him since that day on the highway.

Unlike then, he was glad he could rescue her the night before. Taking her car home was like a part of her going with him. The moment he drove off, he couldn't wait to return the next morning, especially with her scent teasing him inside her car.

Monica's carefree spirit where she was chatty, witty, and animated was thrilling, addictive, and automatically made him a member of #TeamMonica. The woman was fascinating. He glanced at her and remembered the dinner she had prepared. "I woke up this morning still thinking about your leftovers."

She chuckled. "I get my cooking skills from my mom."

"And you can rival a sous chef," he added.

"Thanks, and despite what you witnessed last night and the other time, I'm a courageous soul. My father and my brother instilled that in me." She sighed. "The anxiety attacks make me feel helpless."

He reached over and patted her hand.

"You're a strong, intelligent black woman. I'm happy to be on your team."

The shock on her face preceded the release of her signature laugh. "Me? I'm honored to be part of your team. I applaud the successes of black men beating the odds. Not that you need my accolades, but I'm proud of you anyway."

Wow. "I'm humbled to have your stamp of approval." Her opinion mattered. Tyson swallowed to regroup. "I have to give credit to my Ivy League education."

"I bet you ranked at the top of your class."

While changing lanes, he caught a glimpse of a hero worship expression on her face. "Cum laude, not only was I awarded an academic scholarship, but my skills on the football field earned me an athletic scholarship as well."

"Summa cum laude," she upped him. "BA in mathematics and a minor in business, but you know that from my résumé. And my full ride came in an academic and athletic scholarship too."

Glancing at his passenger, Tyson winked. "Two peas in a pod." He had the same thought about them being dateless on Valentine's Day. He grinned at what he had done because no one sent her flowers.

"What?" She nudged him.

He wasn't about to share that. "Ah, what sports did you play at OSU? Let me guess, basketball, volleyball, or swimming?"

Monica angled her body and faced him. He chuckled at

her mischievous snicker. Whatever she was about to say, he prepared for a tall tale.

"Jump rope," she announced with pride.

Tyson couldn't stop the rumble of laughter escaping from his throat. "Are you serious?" he stuttered, then laughed some more. Her irked expression didn't help as she folded her arms. "Jump rope? How competitive could that be?"

"Try coordinating with three jumpers in Double Dutch and world champions that have performed with the Cirque du Soleil." When she playfully stuck out her tongue at him, Tyson wanted to kiss her. "I know, impressive, huh? Jump rope is considered the perfect fitness regimen. It's a great cardio workout, builds muscles." She paused and slapped his arm as if he wasn't paying attention. His biceps flexed in response. "If you can play tackle in college, I can jump rope."

"Are you challenging my abilities, Miss Wyatt?"

"Nope." She shook her head. "Not when your company signs my paychecks."

He didn't want to be reminded of their business relationship. Unfortunately, their tit-for-tat ended when he parked her car into the same spot as the day before. Tyson craved more of Monica, over dinner at a nice restaurant instead of in her kitchen. She was the type of woman to make a man break all the rules, but at the end of the day, his baby was Tyson & Dyson Communications and was the relationship that he had to nurture first.

As he was about to get out to open her door, she stopped him. "Do you mind if we go in separately?" She squeezed her lips. "I don't want to start any rumors." Her eyes pleaded for his understanding.

In all honesty, neither did he. Nodding, Tyson handed over her keys. Noting the absence of a ring on her fourth finger reminded him that she once belonged to someone. Whoever her ex was, he wasn't man enough to keep her. Tyson was—he wasn't going there, so he quickly dismissed that thought.

After unlocking his car, he slid behind the wheel and started his engine to kill time, watching Monica gathered her things. Her air of confidence was back in place as a burst of wind propelled toward the door.

The last twenty-four hours had been frightening and enlightening. Although he promised not to fire her because of the episode, he still feared she might cave under pressure without a doctor's examination and medication.

You promised, a whisper tickled his ear.

Yeah, I know. He gritted his teeth, wondering if her attacks were limited to the road. Would they overtake her in an elevator, or in a room full of people, or even while giving a company presentation to a prospective client? Those scenarios concerned him.

He still needed to keep an eye on her, but now, his heart was invested in her. And the evidence of that was waiting inside for her. However, if there were a next time on his watch, he would take her to the ER himself—no buts.

Bring her to Me, God spoke and Tyson trembled.

And how was he supposed to do that? When God didn't answer, he racked his brain. The only person who came to mind was Solae.

After waving at Jennifer and Dennis, Monica made a beeline for her corner cubicle. She almost stumbled at what was on her desk. Her Valentine's flowers were clinging to life, but there was a new delivery. Now things were getting creepy. Had she unknowingly entered into some "win flowers for a year" contest or was she dealing with a stalker?

They had the same florist logo as the other delivery. Hesitation replaced the eagerness she experienced from receiving the roses.

After taking a deep breath and slowly exhaling, she drummed her fingers on the desk, debating how badly she wanted to know the sender. She counted, but didn't make it past three before releasing beautiful red amaryllises from their bondage. "Wow."

Hearing Solae's voice, Monica cranked her neck out of her cubicle to see her coworker talking, possibly through her Bluetooth. Back to the flowers, she reached for the envelope and slipped out the card.

The card read: *You're fearless.* What kind of cryptic message was that? Frowning, she tapped into her mind for possible meanings. It definitely wasn't romantic, simply a morale booster. Who would have known she needed a pick-me-up—Veronica or…Tyson? What about the first delivery? She and Veronica didn't send each other flowers and she and Tyson were barely cordial around Valentine's Day.

After pushing back from her desk, she walked down the hall and knocked on Tyson's door, waited, then peeped her head through the opening. On the phone, he glanced up and gave her a welcoming smile before waving her in. He covered the phone with his hand and mouthed, "Give me a minute," before tilting his head for her to take a seat.

She did, admiring this confident black man work his business. Monica imagined him on a magazine spread, highlighting the quintessential CEO. The man knew how to speak, act, and dress the part. His colorful ties caught her eye. She hadn't seen him wear the same one twice. She liked his fashion statement.

Forcing her eyes away, she scanned his office. Her visits there had been limited to quick questions only when an email would have been too lengthy. She relaxed and took in the warm colors of blues and browns. One wall had white built-in shelves that housed more than books—artwork, framed certificates, awards of accomplishments, and numerous article write-ups. Next to his college graduation photo was that of a football team.

She smirked and glanced back at Tyson who was watching her. Ever since last night, his eyes seemed to twinkle whenever she caught him staring. As if to prove her assessment, he winked as he disconnected the call. Her heart skipped a couple of beats. She wanted to scream, stop doing that, but she happened to like the warm-and-fuzzy feeling the gesture triggered.

Linking his fingers together, he graced her with a grin she doubted any man could duplicate. "May I help you, *Miss Wyatt?*" he teased.

"If you sent me flowers—thank you, if not, I have a stalker and I need security detail at the office."

Tyson chuckled and rocked back in his chair. "Consider me your security detail…and yes, I sent the flowers." He stared. "You are fearless, remember that. You've got this, whatever *this* is."

She blinked, then choked out, "That means a lot coming from you, but I noticed they came from the same florist as the post-Valentine's Day flowers. You know anything about them?" She lifted an eyebrow, mimicking a stern disciplinarian.

Was he acting bashful? "Guilty."

Not expecting that answer, Monica sat speechless. Finally, she stuttered, "Why? You barely liked me!" *Or me you*—but this wasn't about her attitude, he started it.

"Let's just say it was my peace offering before the truce." He grinned again.

Woooo. She wasn't mad, but embarrassed. "And you caught me doting on the flowers and thinking I had a secret admirer." They chuckled together, then she lowered her voice. "The flowers are beautiful, but no more, please. It could make for some uncomfortable conversations with the others."

He picked up a pen and toyed with it. "Do I make you uncomfortable?" he asked, giving her his undivided attention. The eagerness on his face let her know her answer mattered.

"Not anymore," she responded softly and stood to leave. "Thank you for everything—the job, the flowers, and your kindness."

Back in her cubicle, she flopped in her chair. This time when she sniffed her old and new flowers, Tyson's handsome face came into view.

Solae's appearance at Monica's desk startled her. Her friend snickered as she folded her arms. "Back-to-back deliveries...hmmm. Your secret admirer again?"

"Yep." She shooed Solae away. This was one secret Monica planned to keep.

Chapter Eleven

As soon as Monica strutted out of his office, Tyson went in search of Solae and snagged her exiting the ladies' room. "Okay, I'm ready to listen."

Startled, she gave him a side look. "About what?"

"Monica." He did a quick head check and lowered his voice. "What can I do to help her with the attacks?"

"Why?" She straightened her body as if gearing for marching orders. "Did something happen?"

If Solae didn't know about the episode, she wasn't going to hear it from him. "You tell me. She's your friend, but she has been on my mind—" and heart, "lately."

She collapsed against the wall. A slow grin crossed her face as she folded her arms. "Did you know she got more flowers today? Somebody likes her," she said in a sing-song tone as she walked away, not answering Tyson's question.

"Hey," he called after her. "What can I do?"

"Church service starts at eleven o'clock. I'll text you the address. See you Sunday, boss." She giggled and continued on her way.

Monica had stayed at her desk most of the day, so Tyson hadn't seen her leave. He resisted the temptation to drive-by her condo to see if her car was there. That would have classified as stalking. Instead, he and Reggie hung out Friday night at a bar with some friends.

Saturday, his urge to check on her hadn't subsided, but he stuck to his weekly routine of visiting with his parents. While eating his mother's smothered pork chops and greens, he chatted about the black hair ad campaign. Once he finished, he joined his father to watch a college basketball game.

Hours later, as he put on his coat to leave, his mother badgered him about going to church. This time he was ready with a response sure to shock her. "A friend from work invited me, so I decided I would check it out." After cataloguing the expression on his mother's face, Tyson laughed.

"Praise the Lord!" His mother rested a hand over her heart and closed her eyes.

Gail walked through the door and frowned at their mother in a meditating stance. "What's going on?"

Before he could answer, his mother snapped out of the trance and relayed what Tyson had said.

Grinning, Gail blocked his exit. "Are you and Miss Wyatt friends now?"

You have no idea. "Yep."

"Could you be attending the same church with her?" she continued her interrogation.

"How would I know?" he asked, but hoped so. If Solae was working on Monica as she had been working on him, there was a possibility. "I'll be a guest of Solae and her family."

She snapped her fingers. "Oh well. We'll get to that altar sooner or later."

"I'm okay with later." He kissed his mother's cheek and left.

Sunday morning, Tyson woke up early for service. The things he was doing for Monica. Witnessing her distress really put the fear of the devil in him. No woman had gotten him to church, besides his mother when there was some type of special event like "Family and Friends Day," or other gatherings she spearheaded. Somehow, Earline Graham accepted his excuses about football to dodge her other invitations or summons.

I don't.

Tyson froze. He didn't imagine the voice. He remained still as if he was listening for a burglar, but the only sound he heard was his furnace kicking in. It was a good thing he was going today.

In his SUV, his navigation system guided him to Rapture Ready Church, twenty minutes away. The name reminded him of instant foods, and ready to consume. Tyson hoped God wouldn't throw him into a fiery furnace for his no-shows.

He crossed the sizable parking lot to the entrance. He half-expected to see Solae waiting in the lobby. Instead, an usher greeted him.

"I'm a guest of the Kavanaughs. Would you happen to know where that family is sitting?"

"Of course," the male usher responded in a tone indicating he knew everybody and where they sat, or maybe Solae told him she was expecting her boss.

Tyson trailed the man through a set of double doors. The sanctuary wasn't as big as the parking lot, but the pews had few pockets of space. Marching down the aisle, the usher stopped and pointed his gloved hand, cueing Hershel to glance over his shoulder.

The usher dismissed himself as Solae's husband stood and shook Tyson's hand, then scooted down to make room.

He noted the singing was inspiring and the announcements brief. After welcoming visitors, Pastor Reed instructed the congregation to turn to Luke, chapter eight. "This is a book of parables, but when Jesus heals somebody, it's a testimony. In verses forty-three through forty-eight, a woman suffered with a condition that couldn't be explained. For twelve years, doctors could do nothing to stop her flow of blood. That's a long time for disappointment. Just because man doesn't have the answers, doesn't mean there isn't a solution. Sometimes, God is waiting on us to come to Him…"

Monica needs to hear this message! Tyson thought.

"The woman's blood issue was her storm. What are you trying to weather today? Man can predict rain and heat, but sometimes…" he lifted his finger, "…storms aren't in the forecast and they sneak up on us. If we're not prayed up, the storms will beat us down. We don't have to live in torment. Come to the Lord and let Him heal you—physically or mentally."

The pastor paused and scanned the audience as if he was searching…Tyson was convinced for Monica.

"Isaiah 55:11 says, 'My Word that goes forth out of My mouth shall not return unto Me void, but accomplish that which I please, and it shall prosper in the thing whereto I sent it.'" Pastor Reed seemed to fire up the crowd with that scripture.

Soon the preacher closed his Bible. "This is your day to come to God at the altar with your issues. Don't go back home the same way you came in. Impress God with your faith and bring your worries to Him. Do it today." He lifted his hands and everyone stood, including Tyson.

Didn't God tell him to bring Monica to Him? But she wasn't there, so Tyson made up his mind to fill in the gap for her.

One of the many ministers waiting at the altar greeted him with a handshake. "Welcome, brother, what do you want from the Lord today?"

"I'm here on behalf of someone who is struggling. If you can pray for Monica…"

"We can do that, but what about you? Before you can help your friend breathe through her issues, you first have to slip on your own oxygen mask as flight attendants instruct passengers. Let's take care of your needs first."

Needs? He didn't have any. He came for Monica. The

man wasn't hearing him. "I'm not the one who's sick. Monica needs help—"

"Maybe you're not physically, but unless you've repented, been washed in Jesus's cleansing blood, and filled with His Holy Ghost, then you're spiritually sick. That's why Jesus died on the cross."

Tyson sighed and was about to return to his seat when the man gripped his hand, bowed his head, and prayed. Finally, he was getting the prayer for Monica.

"Father, in the name of Jesus, I ask that You bless this brother's good intentions. Jesus, You know what they both need from You. Whatever is keeping them from coming to You, remove the obstacles, give them a mind to repent and receive the fullness of Your salvation and the rest will come in Jesus's name. Amen." He released Tyson's hand and smiled.

"You had to put me in there, didn't you?"

"Of course," the minister said.

After the offering and benediction, Tyson said his goodbyes to Solae's family, hoping that wherever Monica was this morning, the prayer had kicked in.

Monica and Veronica mingled with the crowd at the African American Women's Tea Sunday brunch and fashion show. Although it was an annual fundraiser for various high school scholarship funds, this was their first time attending.

"Girl, do you know how many New Year's resolutions we've kept besides this one?" Monica asked as she admired the balloon decorations throughout the room.

Veronica shrugged, then began to count on her fingers. "Let's see, there were five and we were supposed to give each a try at least for two months."

"Nope, six. This counts toward our 'going to social gatherings.'" They secured seats at a random table and removed their coats; the two headed toward the buffet table.

She eyed Veronica's small plate piled with more pastry than fruit. She nudged her friend. "Number one, we were supposed to eat healthier."

"Not today, sister." Veronica gave her a murderous scowl. "The healthy part is restricted to five days. Weekends don't count."

"There's enough food for you on the table, so don't bite my head off too." Her friend was the one who suggested adding diet and exercise on their list, whining about the twenty pounds she had gained last year, blaming it on worrying about Alexander's well-being while serving his country.

Without saying another word, Monica grabbed two muffins from the mountain of treats. She added more fruit than cheese to complete her selection.

Veronica backtracked to the meats. "Besides, our *hair* is healthy. We've been rocking our natural 'dos since December and I'm thinking I may keep this resolution. There is no going back to chemicals for a while," she stated, adding an extra slice of bacon to her stack.

Monica agreed with her on that one. Her fine shoulder-length hair appeared fuller and thicker in its natural state. She disagreed with the food ideology and closed her eyes to the temptation. Of all the meals, she enjoyed breakfast too, but would forgo the meats in favor of the carbs from the oversized muffins.

Neither of them were petite; but they weren't plus size either. Veronica's pounds went to her shapely hips, which she overemphasized in a sway passing a table of seemingly interested male guests.

When they made it back to their table, the other occupants were four ladies. Too bad. Another one of their resolutions was double dating, which Veronica used to try to convince herself she was over Alexander and ready to move on.

They each blessed their food and dug in. Monica took a

sip from her water glass. "So is double dating still on the list?" She smirked.

"Nah," Veronica said after a couple of bites of bacon. "Not on the list. My heart hasn't been in that resolution. You're on your own, sister."

"Hmmm-mmm." She lifted an eyebrow. "I wish you and my brother would kiss and make up instead of all this breaking up."

The two were in denial. They had been childhood sweethearts, but both felt they had outgrown each other. When they dated other people, each complained something was missing.

Would the onset of the anxiety attacks keep her away from a special someone? An episode almost cost her a job and compromised her driving. If a man wasn't already invested in her, he would label her crazy even if she weren't hearing voices.

Tyson's face flashed before her eyes, but she blinked him away. Although she felt a connection with him, she wondered if he felt it too, or if it was her imagination. She wasn't going there. Not only was he her boss, he knew her weakness.

Solae said Monica needed to pray, and she had. She nudged Veronica. "What about reconnecting with church? You stood me up on the first Sunday."

After swallowing a mouthful of bacon, Veronica nodded. "Yeah, you're right. Let's make that happen after our shopping spree to Chi-town next weekend. You said that Black Firefighters Ball your company is attending is formal and we have to make an entrance."

"Too bad you're not into the double dating resolution anymore, because my coworker Solae practically guaranteed there's more handsome hunk firefighters to be had at the ball. And I have to say her husband is fine." Monica fanned her face. "Whew. Hot fine." She giggled, teasing her friend.

"Hmm. I may have to reactivate that resolution." They laughed as the program got underway with handsome male models gracing the runway.

Chapter Twelve

Monday morning, Monica decided her Valentine's flowers had run their course, so she carried them to the kitchen to dump them and rinse out the vase before she started her day.

She caught Mrs. Coates scolding Reggie and Tyson for helping themselves to bagels as she tried to arrange them on the platter. "Oh, good morning, dear." Mrs. Coates saw her first. "If you want one, you better hurry before these greedy bears…" she tilted her head toward their bosses, "eat everything. If they got themselves some wives, they would have a decent meal in the morning," she fussed, causing both of them to groan.

Monica squeezed her lips. She had nothing to add to that conversation as she stepped to the trash bin.

"Wait!" Mrs. Coates startled her. "You're not about to throw them out, are you?"

Without verifying, Monica could feel Tyson's eyes on her. Was he waiting for her answer? "They are pretty much dead." Then added for his hearing, "But they were beautiful."

"Give them to me," the woman ordered. "Once I dry them out, you'll be able to start a dried bouquet in that vase." Taking them, she wrapped them in a paper towel and went back to her desk.

A cute ringtone sounded and Reggie answered, "Hey, babe…" His voice faded as he strolled out of the room. His face lit up whenever he mentioned Tracee's name. Monica looked forward to meeting her at the annual Black Firefighters Ball next week.

At the sink, rinsing the vase, the hairs on Monica's neck began to tinkle. She suspected Tyson was nearby. She proved to be correct when she heard him filling his mug with coffee.

He leaned against the counter beside her and sipped from his cup.

Feeling a playful streak, she ignored him, but his silent assessment was throwing her off. Finally, Monica faced him and wished she hadn't. The man had the most seductive stare. Steadying her breathing, she stared back, lifting an eyebrow in a challenge to get him to cave—it didn't work.

Tyson only intensified his gaze until his nostrils flared. She broke eye contact, only to breathe, before looking at him again. "Yes-s."

"Did you have a good weekend?" he asked in a low husky voice.

"I did."

"No…" he paused and scooted closer, "you know…no incidents?"

Monica's heart twisted. "Will you always bring that up every time you look at me?" She patted her chest as she felt herself fuming. "I wish you, of all people, hadn't seen it."

Whatever his answer, she didn't wait to hear it. She marched out the room, breaking a kitchen rule of not leaving any items in the sink. Well, Tyson could pitch the vase for all she cared.

In her haste, Monica nearly bumped into Reggie. "Sorry," she mumbled, but kept going. If the panic attacks didn't cause her death, the humiliation would.

"Man, what did you say?" she heard Reggie ask him.

Safely inside her cubicle moments later, she spied an envelope on her chair. Tyson, she guessed. She snatched it, contemplating the trashcan, but threw it in her desk drawer instead.

After taking a series of deep breaths, Monica got to work. With the ever-popular trend in online education, the data had to be on point to target potential students. There was already a cluster of colleges and universities flooding the market. She plugged in zip codes and analyzed households' demographics and their income to determine who would seek higher education or complete their education.

When her eyes began to cross from staring at the numbers, and her stomach growled, she thought it was perfect timing for lunch. Pulling out the drawer to get her purse, the white envelope seemed to be waiting for her. She sighed and reached for the card. *I've been praying for you. I hope it helped.*

No signature was needed. Immediately, guilt caused her heart to sink. Clearly, she had overreacted. Of course if she had read Tyson's note before she saw him in the kitchen, she would have understood his question. Her eyes watered as she admitted she owed him an apology. She knew Solae was praying for her, but Monica had no idea he was a praying man and he had thought enough of her to mention her name in prayer.

Oh, the names she was calling herself at the moment. Even her appetite had deserted her. Still, she needed some fresh air.

Miss Wyatt better watch herself. Tyson scowled, replaying their earlier encounter. He might not fire her because of her mental issues, but he had no problem letting her go because of her attitude.

First, she bites his head off, then Reggie walks in and grinds it into dog food. What did he do except go to church and stand in a line to get prayer for her? He didn't envision his note and inquiry to result in a big blowup.

He had been in his office for hours, trying to keep his mind off of Monica, but how could he not think of her when he and Reggie were depending on her numbers for the Missouri State College proposal? Their inventory of billboard rentals was limited to twenty-five neighborhoods across the metro area, so her analysis had to be precise.

So far her mood swings hadn't compromised any projects, but he couldn't help wonder if she was a ticking time bomb. "Jesus, take the wheel." Tyson grunted. What made him say that? As a matter of fact, he couldn't recall where he heard it. Then it dawned on him, it was the faint ringtone reserved for Solae's children.

He was relieved when Reggie knocked on the door. "Ready for the workshop?"

Tyson stood. "Give me a sec." He began to put his folders away. The workshop was actually a networking seminar the St. Louis Minority Council had put together. More than one hundred people attended and this was one way to learn from other small business owners' mistakes.

After slipping on his suit jacket, Tyson shrugged his shoulders until it draped his frame to his liking. When he thought about Monica, he prayed for her again. This time, she better not to cross his path as he stepped out of his office.

Reggie was already in the lobby. "I'm driving."

Once they were buckled up, Tyson stretched his legs.

"Hey, man. I'm sorry for being hard on you earlier about Monica." He paused, probably waiting to see if Tyson was going to respond, but he wasn't in the mood to revisit the topic. "I've never seen her so mad at you. I thought you two had come to some unspoken agreement. She really does good work and I don't want to lose her to a competitor…"

Tyson clenched his jaw to keep from speaking.

"Ain't no mountain high enough, or valley low enough to keep me from Tracee." Reggie began to sing the old Motown tune.

"Yeah, not even your American Express," Tyson

mumbled while rubbing the hairs on his mustache. "And what does Tracee have to do with this?"

"All I'm saying is you see Monica every day. If you like her, tell her. Don't waste your time fighting it."

"You think I like her in that way?" Tyson shifted in his seat.

"I have eyes." He held up two fingers. "Four, if I wear my contacts."

Tyson had heard enough. Monica was too complicated. "Let's talk shop. The hair chain..."

They arrived at the Hilton Hotel near the St. Louis airport and checked in. After sitting through three hours of seminars and two breakout sessions, they headed back to the office.

The information Tyson had retained was helpful, but he missed so much with his mind drifting back to Monica, especially after a few female business owners made no secret of their interests. Reggie cordially advised them he wasn't available.

Tyson had no story to tell as one question kept revolving in his mind. How deep were his feelings for Monica? Reggie drove into the parking lot, and he got out, saying another prayer that she wouldn't cross his path. His father reared him to be a man and demand respect.

Nodding to Mrs. Coates, he marched to his office and closed the door. Monica was driving him crazy.

He hung his coat on a wall hook, then pulled out his chair. A white envelope was resting on the seat. She had some nerve returning his note. He mumbled a few curse words. Maybe he did need that prayer on Sunday.

After grabbing the envelope, he sat. He gritted his teeth. He didn't have time to deal with her. Tyson ripped the envelope and paused. It wasn't the same card he had given her. It had a scenic picture on the cover. As he slowly opened it, steam seemed to spew from his ears until his anger inflated. *I'm sorry, Tyson. You have been nothing but kind to me. You didn't deserve my attitude and disrespect. Even if you fire me, know I'm sorry.*

He closed the card and swirled his chair around to gaze out the window. So she had come to him while he was away. Tyson smiled. He admired a person for making the first move to apologize. His father had taught him that too, but in this case, he wasn't going to budge.

Rubbing his face, he guessed he should apologize too, even if he didn't know why. He put away her card, then left his office for her cubicle.

Hovering over her desk for a few minutes, he watched her until she noticed him. She jumped and patted her chest. Uncertainty filled her eyes.

Tyson peeped over his shoulder. The only person watching him was Dennis who wasn't within earshot. "I'm sorry," he mouthed.

His heart sank when Monica looked as if she was about to cry. "And you're not fired." He couldn't, not when her soulful eyes seemed worried.

"Thank you," she said and relaxed.

He turned to leave but suddenly twirled around and grinned. "Next time, read my note first."

She laughed out loud and the sound caressed his ears. She lowered her lashes. "How did you know I hadn't?"

He didn't answer, but winked and retraced his steps back to his office. It took all day, but finally, the prayer had kicked in.

Chapter Thirteen

Realization hit that Tyson didn't get what he wanted from Monica, so he did a U-turn. This time when he approached her desk, he caught her sniffing his floral arrangement.

The look of tranquility on her face made him hate to disturb her, but he wasn't turning back now. Her lids fluttered open and, as if sensing his presence, she met his stare. "Hi again." She smiled.

"Have dinner with me."

"Yes," she answered softly. "When?"

"I can't wait until tomorrow, or even this weekend. It has to be tonight."

"Tonight?" She blinked. "You do realize it's a work night and by the time I get home and change to go out, it'll be seven o'clock."

He had to think fast. He craved more of the one-on-one time they shared in the car. "I'm game if you are. We can eat some place near your home, and I'll have you back by ten." He checked his watch. "It's four now. Can whatever you're working on wait until tomorrow?" When she nodded, he gave her the okay to leave.

"Tyson sent me home," she said, calling Veronica minutes after getting in her car. She tried her best to keep a straight face to string her friend along.

"What do you mean?" She sounded alarmed. "Please tell me that jerk didn't renege and let you go."

"Well sort of." She giggled. "He thought I could use the extra time for our date tonight." She braced for Veronica's response, and as expected, her friend didn't disappoint.

She screamed her delight. "Woooo! I'll get you for that, so start with he said what, what you said, and don't leave anything out!"

Monica described the blowup in the kitchen, the card, and their apologies. "I didn't see this coming." Veronica asked so many questions, it took the entire drive home to answer them.

Like a mad woman, she hurried into her closet to find something to wear before jumping into the shower. She was dressing when her mother called. Ollie had no idea she had been home for more than an hour.

"Hey, sweetie. How was your day?"

"For a Monday, it was better than expected." Should she mention the date? Knowing her mother, she would start crying, ready to order wedding invitations, and her father would load his shotgun. Until she knew the significance of the dinner, she would keep her mother in the dark.

They chatted a few minutes until her mother rushed Monica off the phone. "*Wheel of Fortune* is about to come on. You have a good night."

"I will," she replied, thinking about Tyson. "You too."

An hour later, her doorbell rang as she slipped her feet into her boots. She opened the door to see Tyson had changed and he was smiling.

"Ready?" He checked his watch and grinned. "Our time is tickin'."

Monica chuckled and grabbed her coat. She'd barely locked the door when Tyson took her hand and hurried her to his SUV. His excitement was contagious.

"If you like Asian food, then we can do Stir Crazy, since it's close."

"I love Asian food." The restaurant was less than two miles down the street.

"Good to know. So, Miss Wyatt, how was your day?" His eyes twinkled with mischief as he tried to keep a straight face once they were on their way.

"Unusual, to say the least." She smirked and glanced out the window.

"Is your boss treating you okay? Let me know if he isn't and I'll have a talk with him."

She burst with laughter and he did too. Once she quieted, she faced him. "My boss is a sweetheart," she said softly.

The air stilled as they stared at each other. She wondered what he was thinking. She wanted to scream, "I'm on a date! I'm on a date!" It had been so long, and never with someone as handsome as Tyson.

Less than ten minutes later, they arrived at the restaurant. In the parking lot, a gust of wind ruffled her hair, so she tightened her scarf around her neck.

Seemingly in tune with her, Tyson quickened their steps to the door. After they were seated and given menus, Monica suggested, "Let's build our own stir fry?" They made their way to the buffet bar to choose their meats, veggies, and spices. Next, the couple waited in line to hand the chefs their add-ons.

While watching their meals be stir-fried, Tyson leaned closer and whispered, "Thanks for the card. It made my day."

When she turned to look up at him, their faces were so close she could smell his minty toothpaste. She blinked before he drew her into a daze. "I really am sorry."

He grinned. "I like calling truces with you."

She smiled and accepted her dish from the chef, so did Tyson. Back at their table, he reached for hands. "Do you mind if we pray?"

"Of course not. I heard it has its benefits."

"Definitely." It wasn't eloquent, but touching, as they said "Amen" in unison.

For the next hour, they quizzed each other about their favorite music, movies, vacations, siblings, until finally Monica asked, "Why me? Why did you ask me out?"

He frowned. "Why not you?"

She pinched her napkin and glanced away. Although she didn't lack self-esteem, she felt defeated with these attacks. She met his eyes again. "You've been privy to my out of control moments, and they ain't pretty. Why would you want to get involved in my drama?"

"Fair question." Tyson shrugged. "That doesn't define you as the woman who fascinates me. Our carpool trip proved there's more to know about you, and I want to."

"I could be crazy, right?" she mumbled and shifted in her seat.

He reached for her hand. "I know no such thing."

Tyson paid the bill while Monica excused herself to the ladies' room. As suspected, a few hours wasn't enough time with her. He had never been in this situation before with a coworker, much less an employee, so he better tame his testosterone.

The drive back to her condo seemed even shorter. Standing on her doorstep, he delivered Monica back minutes before the curfew.

"I had a great time. I like getting to know you, but you have a company to run and I don't want to jeopardize your success. Can we learn how to be friends first and see if there is anything deeper?"

Oh, I'm sure there's something deeper. "I can agree to that."

"Good." She inserted the key and opened her door. "Good night. See you in the morning." She went inside.

Where was his good-night kiss? He joked to himself, staring at the door, then trekked back to his SUV to head home.

Chapter Fourteen

"What do you mean you can't go to the ball?" Monica shrieked over the phone to Veronica. Her friend didn't waste money and the amount they spent on Magnificent Mile in Chicago for the Black Firefighters Ball made Monica question her own sanity over the purchases.

They both had been hyped about attending. Plus, when Tyson asked if he could escort her, she informed him Veronica was technically her date. Plus, them being seen together outside the office would start rumors. "You weren't sick yesterday."

"Yesterday, I thought I had a cold." Her voice sounded weak. "Today, I've been in bed with aches and running a temperature."

"Didn't you get a flu shot?"

"Must have been for the wrong shot, because this one is a monster." She coughed.

"Well, I guess I'm not going either," Monica said, contrary to what she wanted to do, but didn't feel right going without her.

"Go to the ball, Cinderella. I was only your guest, but you're expected to be there." She sneezed and hacked some more.

Monica was getting ill listening to the sound effects. "I'll make an appearance, an hour tops, then leave."

"No, you should stay until the ball ends." Veronica groaned. "Okay, I need more drugs, but text me a picture when you're dressed. I want to make sure you didn't massacre your new contour makeup."

Once they disconnected, Monica padded across her floor to the adjacent bathroom and sat on her vanity stool. As she removed her satin cap, she studied her mass of shiny silky spiral curls, exploding from atop her head. Leaving work early for the hair appointment had been worth it.

She wasn't into heavy eye makeup, but Veronica insisted focusing on Monica's eyes would give her hairstyle a more dramatic effect, so she got busy. She followed the extra steps outlined in her contour pamphlet. Twenty minutes later, she had done it all from her primer to her expertly shaped eyebrows. She stared at her reflection.

Grabbing her smartphone, she clicked a selfie, and sent it to Veronica. When her friend didn't respond, Monica suspected she was wiped out.

Now, as she stood in front of the wall-length mirror, she admired the beaded form-fitting bluish-green dress. Even though it was strapless, she had a short faux fur cape to cover her chest area or she might be sick next. With her toes peeping from her clear shoes, she could be Cinderella. What would Tyson say? *Or think?* She smirked.

She stepped into her chariot—car—and drove off. Thirty-plus minutes later, she arrived at the downtown event where valets were waiting as she parked in the circular drive.

One assisted her out, and another escorted her to the door. The magnificent entrance had an elegant winding stairwell, leading to the second floor ballroom. Opting to take the marble stairs versus the elevator, Monica began her ascend.

As she neared the landing, she heard her name called. Cranking her neck around, she spotted Solae beside her husband, waving. When she reached the level, Solae sauntered her way. "Look at you," they almost said in unison.

"Some firefighter is going to rescue you tonight, girlfriend!"

Monica blushed despite the fact she was developing stronger feelings toward Tyson since the dinner date a week ago. She didn't need flowers or notes from him to be reminded of his attraction. Somehow, whenever they made eye contact, his eyes hinted of his thoughts. And no one at work had a clue what was going on between them.

"Where's your friend?"

"Sick with the flu." She pouted and Solae nudged her toward the entrance of the ballroom.

"That's too bad. Well, come on, I'll introduce you to my sister-in-law. Plus, Reggie's girlfriend, Tracee, is here, so you'll have a chance to meet her if he will release her from protective custody." Monica laughed out loud before she could catch herself and replace it with something more subtle like a dignified giggle.

Solae looped her arm through Monica's, then swept her into the room where there had to be three hundred people easily, yet there was space for mingling. "My husband has plenty of single firefighter friends."

"Hmmm-mmm." Soon she spied Reggie with a woman who could put Cinderella to shame in her stunning attire. "Is that Tracee?" She tried not to point.

"Yes." She yanked on Monica's hand. "If you don't meet her now, you might not."

She caught a glimpse of Solae's husband off to the side, speaking with another man. But his wife was definitely in his view. Would Tyson look at her like that?

"I'm glad you could make it," Reggie said as he pulled his girlfriend closer. "And this gorgeous creature is my lady, Tracee Matthews." He planted a kiss on her cheek and she closed her eyes, seemingly to relish his gift. Not only did they make a stunning couple, the look of love on their faces glowed.

Next, she met Candace, Solae's sister-in-law, and Royce, Hershel's brother. Her friend seemed to be on a mission to introduce her to five eligible bachelors a minute. Monica gave Hershel a silent plea to get his wife.

Relieved, she made her way to the buffet table. The selection was endless. Besides the men, Veronica would hate she missed the food.

After generous servings of a little this and that, Monica snagged an unoccupied counter table. Once she said her grace, she sampled the meatballs and closed her eyes to savor the seasoning. She opened them and glanced around the ballroom. The ambiance was unmatched and there was a nonstop parade of firefighters in uniform, mingling with the guests.

As a matter of fact, one was coming her way when Tyson appeared out of nowhere, and intercepted. His stride was calculated. When her jaw dropped, she was glad that nothing was in her mouth.

His eyes locked with her, reeling her in like catfish. She had often heard a woman describe a man as gorgeous, Tyson wasn't one of them. He was too rugged to be a pretty boy— he was one hundred and ten percent all male with the build to prove it. She thought he was handsome in a suit and tie, but the tux seemed to magnify his every muscle.

"It's about time you got here, Miss Wyatt." He winked. "You are incredibly beautiful." His nostrils flared. Yes, Tyson gave her the attention she craved.

He didn't stop walking until he towered over her. The faint whiff of his aftershave overpowered her senses.

"Thank you." Monica blushed.

Stuffing a hand in his pants pocket, he looked around. "Where's your date?" He smirked and wiggled an eyebrow.

"At home, sick with the flu, and Veronica will hate she missed it."

"I guess I'll have to fill in." He grinned and stole a meatball and she feigned protest. Monica missed his private attention, like now as he seemed content to patiently watch her finish every morsel on her plate. After she dabbed her lips, he grabbed her hand and the tinkling started on contact and traveled up her arm until she shivered.

"Cold?" He looked concerned.

"No."

"Come on, I want you to mingle and meet some of our clients." He leaned closer to her ear. "Plus, I want to get lost in the crowd with you."

Like Tracee had done when Reggie kissed her cheek, Monica closed her eyes and relished in Tyson's declaration.

For the next hour, she was able to put faces to names she had heard staff members mention. Also, Tyson stayed at her side until she excused herself to the ladies' room to freshen up. Minutes later when she strolled out, he was nowhere in sight.

As she peered through the crowd, a sense of fear came over her. She couldn't shake the dread that something was about to happen, and the feeling was building. As if she was the Incredible Hulk, Monica had to get out of there before she turned into a spectacle and embarrassed herself and Tyson.

Evidently, driving wasn't the sole culprit sparking the panic attacks. Did she have to add crowds to the list? Now wasn't the time for her to gather data. If she didn't start for home immediately, she might find herself stranded on a dark highway and that thought did freak her out.

Tyson rounded the corner and his eyes sparkled. "Hey, you."

She tried to keep a steady voice. "I think I'm going to head home." She struggled to smile.

He didn't hide his disappointment. "But it's early. Is everything—" He paused as his gazing intensified.

"Yep. Veronica was supposed to come with me. Since I'm alone I don't want to be out late."

"I can trail you home if you stick around," he offered.

That wasn't an option. She shook her head as her heart pounded and shouted to get out of there fast. "Good night."

"Is everything okay?" he asked, matching her steps beside her toward the entrance.

No, it's not, but she wasn't going to tell him that, so she lied. "Maybe I'm getting a touch of the bug Veronica has."

"Then you shouldn't be driving," he argued, keeping a steady grip on her elbow as he guided her down the winding stairwell.

She handed a valet her ticket. "You stay. I'll text you when I get home, okay?"

"No, that's not okay." His nostrils flared as he frowned.

When her car arrived, she was saved from sparing with him. Tyson tipped the man and shooed him off from opening her door. Perspiration was beginning to line her upper lip as she climbed inside. When she reached for the door, Tyson wouldn't release it.

"I'm praying you get home safely."

"Thanks." She yanked her door shut, shifted into drive, and sped off. "Lord, if You're listening, please help me make it home."

Monica was lying to him. Tyson could sense it. She had avoided eye contact, a hint that she was keeping something from him. He grunted as he folded his arms and watched her taillights until she turned the corner.

Was she having another attack? How was that possible? His heart said to go after her and make sure she was all right. His head said to take her at her word and go back into the ball and take care of his business.

Falling for Monica was making him compromise his ethics. This is what he feared, entering into a relationship with an employee. He huffed and tightened his jaw. Tyson needed to make a decision. He had invested a whole lot of money and time into Tyson & Dyson Communications to leave in the middle of a function. A woman like her, no matter how special she was, could be replaced, right?

Decision made, he spun around to head back to the party at the same time the valet, who he handed his ticket when he placed a tip for Monica in his hand, pulled up in his SUV. He stared at his vehicle. He calculated the time it would take to drive to her condo and come back to the ball.

Since he wouldn't be in a mix-and-mingle mood until he heard from her, Tyson whipped out his cell and sent Reggie a text, although he doubted his friend would take his eyes off of Tracee long enough to read it. Hey, had to make a quick run. Be back before it's over.

He slipped the phone back into his jacket breast pocket, tipped the valet again, and took off after Monica with one hand on the wheel and another struggling to secure his seat belt.

"God, please don't let anything happen to her," he whispered as he got on Highway 40, searching for her car. It didn't take long before he spotted her Mazda 6 in the slow lane, driving under the minimum speed limit. His heart dropped as he sent more prayers up for her safety. The slow speed was as dangerous as someone speeding.

He rubbed his face in frustration. Tyson didn't want to spook her, so he stayed a couple of cars back. He was confused, but relieved when she turned off the highway at the St. Louis Zoo exit, a couple of miles before connecting with I-170 to her house. He followed her on Skinker Boulevard for blocks until he figured out she was taking the streets to her house, but even on the street she kept hitting her brakes.

He wanted to curse out his frustration, but he couldn't do that and pray, so he kept mumbling, "God, keep her safe, let her be okay, and help my sanity."

Monica's twenty-minute drive from downtown to Olivette via highway turned into a forty-minute journey through the city, University City, and finally, Olivette.

Tyson was getting a tension headache. When she reached her complex and parked in the driveway, he considered calling an ambulance, not for Monica, but for himself. His nerves were shot. Since she didn't leave any room in her driveway for him to pull alongside, he blocked her in at the curb and hurried to the driver's side and tugged on the door.

"You followed me," she stated as if she wasn't surprised. "I noticed a vehicle following me and I thought about calling the police, then I recognized you."

"And that wasn't an easy task. I wish you had, because we both could have had our vitals checked." He lifted her out of the car.

She collapsed on his chest, shaking. He scooped her up in his arms and carried her to the front door, then planted her back on her feet. "Baby, what happened back there?" he asked, taking her keys, then opening her door.

She shrugged off her cape as she walked into the house. Closing the door, he followed her to the sofa. "I freaked out." A tear trickled down her cheek.

Please don't cry. Sitting next to her, he willed her not to cry as he wrapped his hands around hers. "How do you feel now? You're still beautiful to me." He smiled and squeezed her hands until he got what he was hoping, she smiled back.

"Better that I'm home."

"Good." He massaged her fingers. "Listen, I don't know what caused you to have an attack." Rubbing her hands and staring into her dazed eyes that pleaded with him—for help, understanding, what? She was his damsel and his heart.

Tyson had broken so many rules with his attraction to Monica, but he was willing to risk one more. "Do you think a kiss would trigger them?"

Brightness replaced the darkness in her eyes and she leaned closer. "I don't think so."

Sweeping her into his arms, he kissed her gently. He brushed kisses against her lips to convey that everything would be all right. When she pulled away, Tyson didn't release

92

her. He rubbed her back, coaxing her to rest her head on his chest.

After a few minutes, he reluctantly loosened his hold. He cupped her cheek with his hand and immediately felt the softness of her skin. Only Monica could make him debate everything as he got lost in her eyes. "I have to get back to the party, but if you need me to stay, I will."

She lowered her lashes and nodded. Tugging her to her feet, he walked backward to the door, gently pulling her with him. "So we're clear. The kiss means you belong to me." He winked and reached for the doorknob.

"Expect flowers in the morning." He stole one more kiss. "Good night." He exhaled before trekking back to his SUV. One thing he failed to tell her was he was probably in love with her, but that declaration might trigger something within him—fear that he was going down.

Chapter Fifteen

Was it her imagination, or was her crisis drawing her and Tyson closer? Monica wondered the next morning. Before she could call to check on Veronica and get her take, her phone rang. "Hey, I was thinking about you. Feeling any better?"

"My fever broke during the night, but I don't have the strength to get out of bed." She sounded weak. "How did last night go, Cinderella?"

She finger-combed the tight curls in her hair and wandered into her living room. "The good news, you missed plenty of food, fine firefighters—"

"Uh-uh, that sounds like bad news to me."

Monica shook her head. "Me having another crisis was definitely the bad news of the night."

"Oh-no."

"I know. The panic attacks are getting out of hand, but Tyson kissed me and made it better." She grinned.

"What!" Her strength seemed to come to life. "I missed everything, and I hate to hear about these anxiety episodes, but something good did come out of it, kind of, right?"

"I think so, which is what I wanted to ask you. Instead of the attacks chasing him away, he's meeting them head on. Confusing, huh?"

"No, sister, it's romantic."

"So you don't think he considers me a charity case? I mean, this isn't the ideal attraction."

"*Hmph.* I'll be his 501(c) (3). He's the type of man every woman is waiting for and to know he's praying for you through this, you should be laying out your Sunday best now. Tyson Graham is a keeper." Her voice cracked. "And this was the weekend we were going to church. I hate to bail out on you again."

"Nah, don't worry about it. I might go by myself again. I know Solae would be glad to see me. Get some rest. I'll make you some homemade soup and bring it over."

"No, you rest today. I'm really concerned about you too. If you don't get a handle on whatever is freaking you out, you won't be able to drive to the corner, leave the house, or God knows what else."

"I know, hurry up eight more weeks." Monica prayed she could hold off that long.

"You are too independent for your own good, girl! If Tyson wants to spend his money on you in that way, let him. Ooh…" She paused. "My tooth, my back is aching, and I think I need to see a foot doctor. You think he's got me covered?"

"You're crazy." She chuckled, then sobered as she ended their call. Truth be told, last night did damage Monica's psyche big time. But she'd only experienced that feeling while in her car. Now, she'd been out in public. What next? "God, I'm scared," she mumbled, staring at her reflection in a wall mirror. "Really afraid." She was about to cry. No kiss, no matter how good the kisser, could erase that feeling of detachment from her surroundings.

I am the Great Physician, she heard His whisper. *I heal the body and soul.*

"Then heal me please," she pleaded as the doorbell rang. Half hoping, half expecting Tyson to be on the other side, Monica hurried to answer. Flowers greeted her instead. Her heart warmed, forgetting he'd mentioned sending them and he had.

"Thank you," she told the delivery man and offered to give him a tip if he would wait, but he declined.

"Mr. Graham made the delivery worth it." He jogged back to his truck.

After closing the door, she carried them to the kitchen counter. She tore the wrapping away and reached for the card. *We'll get through this together. Promise. Call me when you're up to it. Hugs and kisses.*

She was in awe at his commitment to her. Inspired by his words, she called him.

"Did you rest well?"

"Yes." She paused. "Thank you for leaving the ball and coming to see about me. Words can't begin to describe how special you made me feel."

"You have no idea how special you are. Asking you out was a game changer for me. No other woman has gotten to me like you."

She smiled, flattered, and fingered a flower petal. "Is that a bad thing?"

"I'll never regret how we met. Will you include me in your plans today?"

Monica nodded before answering him. "I'm not doing much except cook Veronica soup and take it to her." When he asked where she lived, she assured him not far. "Ten minutes tops." On a good day, but after the scare last night, she might need extra time. She didn't tell him that.

"How about I bring sandwiches to go along with the soup and I drive you? Please don't fight me on this. I don't want you behind the wheel today."

"Is this my boss talking?"

"No, this is from your man. See you soon." He disconnected before she could protest.

Tyson had prayed throughout his restless night for Monica, because she was fighting an enemy she couldn't see. He also had never told a woman he loved her, but he was close to professing it. Once he said it, there would be no turning back. But her episodes couldn't be ignored, no matter how much he tried to push them to the back of his mind.

He needed to vent. As close as he was to Reggie, he doubted his business partner and best friend could be objective when it came to Monica. Reggie liked her from day one. Plus, he didn't know the demons she was fighting.

By default, his father was the other option. He was a good listener above his other qualities. "How you doin', Pops?" he asked when he answered. After they exchanged the standard greetings, Tyson was blunt.

"I like this woman, really like her, probably love her, if I'm honest, but she has a condition and I don't know how that will affect our relationship down the road. Will she get better or worse?" he rambled on until he had to catch his breath.

"A medical condition?"

Tyson sighed in frustration. "Until she sees a doctor, I think it could be mental—I don't know." That frustrated him as he paced his living room floor.

Seconds ticked by while he waited for his father to say something. "There are drugs for conditions, son. We can never judge a person by conditions. I have high blood pressure. No one would know it because I take medicine and it's controlled. If her mental issues can be controlled with meds, then it's up to you to accept that or move on."

Drugs or no drugs, Tyson didn't want to accept it. If he hadn't seen it with his own eyes, he probably wouldn't believe it. "I was hoping for more of a 'stay or run to the hills' answer."

His father chuckled. "When people are stressed, things happen to their bodies and minds. My advice is if you care about this woman, help her get the help she needs. If it works out, you'll be glad you did. If it doesn't, at least you can say you tried."

"You're right. Thanks, Pops." Tyson disconnected and closed his eyes. He took a few minutes to digest the options his father outlined.

When he left his place, Tyson detoured to the closest Cecil Whitaker, a St. Louis chain known for its pizzeria, and he ordered three sub sandwiches, in case her friend had an appetite.

Less than an hour later, he knocked on Monica's door. She greeted him with the sweetest smile. There was no way he could desert her. He meant what he said earlier about working through her problem together. "Hey, whatever you have smells good," he said, crossing the doorway and handing over the bag.

"Thank you for my flowers. They're beautiful."

"You're welcome." Once he removed his coat, he opened his arms. "Come here. I think we both need a hug." As he rested his chin on the top of her head, Tyson closed his eyes and reflected on the previous night's crisis. *What a difference a day makes.*

She seemed content to let him hold her. When she pulled away, the seduction in her eyes made him swallow. Then he realized she wasn't purposely flirting.

"Come on, the soup's ready." She led him to the kitchen and placed the bag on the table and began to take out the sandwiches. "You're eating two of these monsters?" She chuckled.

"No, one is for your friend."

"Aww, how thoughtful. When it comes to food and Veronica, you've gained a friend for life."

"Do you need help?" He was ready to pitch in.

"Nope. Wash your hands and have a seat." She scooped soup into one bowl and handed it to him along with a bottled water. "Unless you want soda or juice."

"I'm good," he said, waiting for her to join him. When

she did, he reached across the table. Instead of gathering her hands in his, he looped his fingers through hers. "God, thank You for this food and this beautiful creature coming into my life. Lord, help her help us to get through this. In Jesus's name. Amen."

When he opened his eyes, Monica's lids fluttered until they revealed her eyes glazed over. "Thank you," she choked out.

"Always."

"That was a nice prayer."

But was it enough to release you from this crazy nightmare? he debated.

Keep praying, God answered.

And Tyson planned to. He tasted her chicken soup and smacked his lips. "*Hmp, hmp, hmp.*" He shook his head. "What can't you cook?"

"Nothing, as long as I have a recipe." She bit into the sandwich and nodded. "This is good." She wiped her mouth. "About last night…"

"Yeah, about last night." He was waiting for her to bring it up as he took her hand. "You didn't trust me, not enough to tell me something was wrong." When she opened her mouth, he shook his head. "No, Monica, I need to say this. I care about you, which makes me worry. Please don't ever lie to me again."

"I won't," she whispered.

"Last Sunday when I attended church, it was for you. It was my way of standing in the gap. Silly, huh?" He chuckled. "After hearing a sermon about healing, I'm convinced God can do the same for you, but you've got to come to Solae's church and hear what I heard for you to understand. I can't go on seeing you tormented like this, so will you come with me?"

"No."

He blinked at her lack of hesitation in answering.

Her lips curled into a smile. "I had planned to go myself, so will you come with me?"

Tyson exhaled. She had him going for a second. "You didn't have to ask." He guided her face to his and sealed it with a kiss.

Chapter Sixteen

Veronica screamed and slammed her door in front of Monica and Tyson's faces, but not before grabbing the container of soup and sandwich.

From inside, she shouted, "Monica, I'll kill you when I regain strength! Thanks for the soup." There was a pause before she continued. This time, her tone was nicer. "Hi Tyson, thanks for taking care of my girl. I'll meet you when I'm at my best."

He had seemed amused at her antics, and replied, "I look forward to it."

Later that night over the phone after Veronica gave her a tongue-lashing, she gave her a stern warning to hold on to that man. Monica didn't argue, but it seemed more like Tyson was holding on to her. He was the type to introduce to her parents, and with that thought, she drifted off to sleep.

Sunday morning, Monica was in good spirits about attending church with Tyson. She donned a black turtleneck, a long black skirt, and accented it with a colorful scarf before fitting her curls under a black fedora. It was too cold to look cute, but she tried.

When Tyson arrived, the first thing she spotted was a medium-sized Bible. "For you." He leaned closer. "And this."

PAT SIMMONS

He brushed a kiss against her lips. "I didn't know if you had a Bible or preferred to read on your tablet or phone, but…"

She placed a finger to his lips, which he kissed. "I'll cherish the words in it and the man who gave it to me." When Monica lifted her coat off the hook, not only did Tyson help her with it, but he spun her around and buttoned it.

She laughed. "You know I'm capable of doing that."

"Yep, and I'm very capable of taking care of you too." He grabbed her hand and tugged her out the door. Once she locked it, he tightened his grip to keep her from slipping on some icy patches.

This was day three of spending time together outside of the office, and she enjoyed every minute of it. Monica didn't look forward to returning to work in the morning where their relationship would be restricted to business only.

"Hey, you're too quiet over there." He patted her hand while they waited at a stoplight.

"Just thinking."

"I'll listen whenever you're ready to share."

Smiling, Monica cleared her head. "Nothing deep." So she chatted about nothing serious until he turned into Rapture Ready Church's parking lot.

"Did you tell Solae we were coming?" Tyson asked.

"Nope."

"Then she'll be pleasantly surprised."

In the foyer, a male usher seemed to recognize Tyson and nodded. Taking her hand, he followed the direction of the usher to a pew where Solae was sitting with her children. Hershel was absent, probably on duty at the firehouse.

Glancing over her shoulder, Solae did a double take before grinning wildly, then she scooted down to make room for them. "Yay." Solae squeezed her lips as if to keep her excitement from escaping. "It's about time he told you how he felt."

"You knew?" Monica wiggled in her seat so he would have plenty of room on the pew.

102

"Yep." Her coworker stood and began to clap along with others to the beat of the song.

Monica and Tyson got on their feet too and sang along with the words flashing on a large screen. Solae lightly bumped her, but kept singing. Closing her eyes, she allowed the chorus to penetrate her spirit. She was disappointed when the singers yielded the floor to the man who identified himself as Pastor Reed.

"I welcome all first-time and returning visitors today," the preacher said.

Tyson squeezed her hand and guided her to her feet when the pastor asked guests to stand to be acknowledged. Solae and her tribe must have clapped and yelled the loudest.

She was surprised Pastor Reed didn't waste any time with his sermon.

"There is a war going on today, right now, and for some of you, right here in this place of worship, and God has equipped His saints with armor that we're not using. My text is from 2 Timothy 1:7. Verse seven says, 'For God hath not given us the spirit of fear; but of power, and of love, and of a sound mind.'"

Sound mind? Her heart skipped. The other night she thought she was losing her mind. She was so afraid.

"The Bible says, 'For we wrestle not against flesh and blood, but against principalities, against powers, against the rulers of the darkness of this world, against spiritual wickedness in high places.' For those of you who are taking notes, you can find it in Ephesians 6:12, a warning scripture. We're reminded to fight a battle others might not see. Once we receive the Holy Ghost, God gives us a spirit of faith and it's faith that battles with and defeats fear."

Monica felt as if she was being overpowered again, right there in church, but unlike before, instead of gaining strength, something held it at bay.

"Fear is of the devil and its target is your mind and your mind controls your thoughts, which influences your actions that can trigger suicide attempts, depression, worry, hallucinations, voices, and other devices of spiritual warfare. The sins of this world have invaded our hearts and minds. Suit up!" he shouted and his words echoed through the sanctuary like a ripple effect.

Again her heart responded as if she was with child and the baby was kicking her. She looked at Solae who seemed to be in her own zone with her eyes closed, rocking back and forth. Clearly, she was meditating. To her right, Tyson was watching her. She smiled and refocused on the sermon. "You all know the armor of God can't be penetrated. Suit up with your shield of faith outlined in Ephesians 6…"

Monica analyzed the message as if she was adding numbers for demographics. She needed this spirit, which would give her power and most of all, the sound mind.

Every time Pastor Reed shouted, "suit up," there was a roar in the sanctuary, reminding her of being on the winning team at a football game.

The experience was energetic and powerful, but she felt Pastor Reed left her on a cliff when he closed his Bible and asked all to stand. Twisting her lips in a pout, she wanted more.

"The time has come for you to make a decision about whose side you're on. When fear comes knocking at your door, summon your faith to answer it. If you want the spirit of God in your life today, first repent of your sins and then come to the altar where the ministers will pray for you. Go all the way with God and let the Blood of Jesus wash away your sins. God will fill your clean empty vessel with His Spirit, so there will be no room for the devil to inhabit. He'll speak to you in heavenly tongues." He stretched out his arm. "Will you come today?"

Monica didn't need to be asked again and she turned to nudge Tyson out of the way. As she walked to the altar, she sensed his presence beside her. He waved a minister over, bypassing other ministers who were closer to them.

"This is my Monica. I asked you to pray for her," Tyson said.

My Monica? She was humbled by his possessiveness. The minister nodded. "Hi, Monica, and I'm glad to see you back, brother. What do you want from the Lord today?"

"The works. I want to be saved, I want the Holy Ghost and the armor…" She ran out of breath with her list for God until tears ran down her cheeks.

"Have you repented?" the minister asked and she nodded. She'd repented of everything, or at least everything that she could remember, even white lies. "Do you consent to be baptized for the remission of those sins?"

She nodded again, then the man eyed Tyson.

"You brought your friend today, but what about you? God is waiting on you to come to Him for yourself."

When Tyson acted as if he wasn't budging, she reached touched his arm. "Hey, if you believed God enough for me, believe Him for you."

"Right." Bowing his head, she followed Tyson's lead and allowed the minister to lay hands on them and pray.

Next, they were separated into dressing rooms. An older women instructed her to change clothes to be baptized. "You look awfully nice, sugar. I guess we'll say you wearing black today is to bury your sinful nature. Once you come out of the water, you'll be white as these clothes." She handed Monica clothing and stepped out to give her privacy to completely undress.

Suited in the white garments, swimming caps, plus white socks, she was ready to receive this promise of the Holy Ghost. When she didn't see Tyson at the pool deck, she hoped he hadn't backed out, but with or without him, she was going all the way with God.

She cautiously stepped into the water, never having learned how to swim. Another minister gripped her hand and helped her down the couple of stairs, then she was told to fold their arms across their chests.

Her heart pounded with excitement about the unknown. She closed her eyes and wondered if church had been dismissed, because the once-noisy sanctuary was quiet.

"My dear sister, upon the confession of your faith, and the confidence we have in the blessed Word of God, concerning His Death, Burial, and Resurrection, we now indeed baptize in the name of Jesus, for there is no other name under Heaven that can save you for the remission of your sins, and Acts 2:38 says you shall receive the gift of the Holy Ghost. Amen."

She was submerged under the water for seconds, but when she resurfaced, she felt lighter, as if physical baggage had been left behind. The silence in the sanctuary was replaced with roars of jubilation. Evidently, the baptisms were the main attractions. She lifted her hands in praise as tears rolled down.

"Come on, baby," the same woman said, draping a warm towel over her shoulders and guided her back into the changing room. "Let's get you out of these wet clothes. Don't worry about putting back on your black. That's only the outer garment; your soul is whiter than snow."

Again, she gave her privacy to dry off and change.

"Now, let's get you in the prayer room and let the Lord fill you with Tongues of Fire like He did in the Book of Acts. That Holy Ghost is something powerful!"

Monica grinned. "I'm ready to get everything God has for me." Once she got that Holy Ghost, she could fight fire with fire.

Only I can save her, God whispered to Tyson as he changed for the baptism. That wasn't the only scolding the Lord gave him before he stepped foot in the pool. *Any man who comes to Me must come in spirit and in truth. Come to Me for yourself only.*

Tyson had trembled with overwhelming fear that God

knew his every thought, which included his nonchalant attitude toward church commitment. He had been too rebellious as a child to want to be baptized, because he was never sorry for his mischievous deeds. Seeing how much Monica needed God caused Tyson to realize he needed Jesus just as much. It was at that moment he truly repented of his sins.

Now as he sat in the small chapel area, waiting for the Lord to give him this Tongue of Fire, he pushed Monica to the back of his mind and prayed for God to take control of *his* life.

Others had joined him in the room, but he refused to be distracted. Some mumbled, others were more vocal as they prayed, but Tyson drowned them out with his own petitions, until suddenly, there was a sound like a tornado heading their way. An explosion seemed to shake the room, punching him in the gut.

He heard others speak in a language that didn't sound as if it was from this planet. Seconds later, his jaw moved on its own volition and utterings spilled out of his mouth. Tyson knew it in his soul. He had received the Holy Ghost. When God gave him a space to say something, he shouted, "Hallelujah."

Tyson never imagined he would shut the church down, but apparently, a couple of deacons were waiting for the last candidates to receive the Holy Ghost before locking up the church until night service.

There hadn't been one person in the prayer room who hadn't spoken in other tongues. Even now, half hour later, on the parking lot, many of them were still rejoicing as he helped Monica into his SUV. "That was amazing!" she said, buckling her seat belt. "That has to be one of God's best kept secrets."

He agreed, starting the engine. "I guess it is if we don't read our Bibles."

As he drove anyway to take Monica to brunch, she began to cry and speak in tongues as she worshiped Jesus. Fifteen minutes later, when he parked outside First Watch café, they praised God together.

This by far, had been the best day in his thirty-six years. His salvation had been a game changer.

Chapter Seventeen

"Aren't you glowing?" Mrs. Coates stated the obvious, grinning from ear to ear as Monica glided into the lobby on Monday morning.

Yes, I am. She had the man—Tyson—and now she had the man who died for her—God. She twirled around. "I'm happy."

"Yep, love does that to you." She sighed.

She paused and considered Mrs. Coates' assessment. "You're right. I'm in love with Jesus!"

"Honey, I was talking about you and Tyson." She frowned. "I saw the way he hovered over you at the ball, then disappeared when you left…"

Was there anything this woman didn't see? "My happiness today is because Jesus saved my soul yesterday."

"Oh, okay. That's nice, dear, but I thought it had to do with Tyson strolling in here not long ago with a similar bounce as you. He was whistling and winked at me—he never does that! Plus, he was carrying a gift. He didn't give it to me…" she rambled.

Tyson had informed her about a morning meeting that he and Reggie had to attend. However, she didn't think he would stop by the office first. "Thanks for the heads up." She continued on her way.

Monica barked out her laugh, then slapped her hand over her mouth when she spied the gift centered on her seat. Mrs. Coates had to have 20/20 vision to zoom in on a box small enough to fit in the palm of her hand.

"And when did you do this, Mr. Graham?" she mumbled and removed the lid. Her heart fluttered as she lifted a silver chain with a small heart dangling from it. *ME* was engraved on one side, *YOU* was on the back. She smiled, reading the enclosed note: *This goes with the Valentine's flowers.* It was March and he was still stuck in February.

Solae appeared, rubbing her hands. "When did you get here? I saw Tyson leaving your desk as I was coming in, so what you get?"

"Is nothing secret around here?" She displayed the necklace.

"Nope. It's beautiful." She grabbed Monica's hands. "I'm glad you responded to God's call for salvation at church yesterday. The Bible says God delights in doing great things for His children, so God is going to do mighty works in your life."

"I hope so." She forced back the doubt the devil was tapping at her mind. No, God gave her sound mind and she would fight to keep it.

After a few encouraging words, Solae returned to her desk and Monica started inputting more than one hundred zip codes to get the demographics on which households would be prospective online students. At noon, she mouthed to Solae, who was on the phone, "I'm going to lunch."

In the kitchen, she warmed leftovers from Sunday's dinner she had with Tyson. She missed his presence now. Of all the days for him to be away, it had to be the day after God saved them. She hadn't realized she was smiling until Solae snuck up on her.

"It's good to see you relaxed and happy. You and Ty make a cute couple."

"Thank you and yes, I am happy." She giggled. "After

seeing how Hershel adores you, I didn't think I would ever find a man who looked at me like that." She paused, ashamed of what she was about to confess. "To be honest, I was kind of a little jealous of you."

"Me?" Solae frowned and chuckled.

"I know it was silly, but what woman wouldn't be envious when she sees a woman with a perfect life: three beautiful children and a gorgeous husband."

Solae retrieved her lunch sack from the fridge, unzipped the cover, and exhaled. "We have to work hard not to be jealous of what someone else has, especially a sister in Christ, when we don't know their testimony. God is the giver of gifts if we ask for them."

Didn't God say something like that to her? She eyed her friend scrutinizing the contents. "What's wrong? Isn't that your lunch?"

"Oh, it's mine all right. My children seem to get a kick out of fixing Mommy lunch, so I eat what they prepare—or try, even if they smear two inches of peanut butter with a trace of jelly on a piece of bread. It's the thought that counts, right?" Solae grinned. "Ready to pray?"

"I've been waiting on you." She bowed her head.

"Lord, in the name of Jesus, thank You for my dear sister's salvation and this food my children prepared with sweet hearts. Please sanctify and remove all impurities, especially if they didn't wash their hands…"

Opening one eye, Monica looked at her with amusement, then closed it again.

"And please let us be mindful of those who are hungry and bless them in Jesus's name."

"Amen," they said in unison.

While Monica dug into her Caesar salad, Solae got up and washed her apple. Sitting again, she unwrapped her sandwich. One slice was wheat, the other was white. They both snickered. "I've got to love them."

After biting into the cookie dough-thick sandwich, Solae

washed it down immediately with long sips from a kids-size juice box. "Ah. Now, what you see with me is the result of Jesus taking the wheel, or the lead, in our lives. I couldn't have children, which had been a deal breaker in my relationships, even with Hershel. I loved that man so much, but I ended it before he did." Her eyes watered and she blinked. "It doesn't appear your episodes are enough to make Tyson walk away."

"Wait a minute. Those aren't your children?" Monica's mouth dropped open.

Solae lifted her chin. "I didn't birth any of them, but they are my children. I love them, care for them, and I'm their mother. The boys are from Hershel's first marriage and little Hershey, I adopted her after Hershel and I broke up, but I think that little girl brought us back together. She is a daddy's girl and a typical little sister." She scrunched up her nose at the sandwich before taking another bite. "So the perfection you see is God's handiwork."

"Wow," Monica said in disbelief. "Maybe Tyson and I can survive an office romance and the attacks."

"Yep." She wrapped up the sandwich and threw it in the trashcan. "Girl, I tried, but one box of juice won't cut it and I can only drink so much water with one sandwich." She walked to the freezer and retrieved a frozen entree, then twirled around, grinning. "Backup."

They laughed and filled the rest of their lunch hour taking about the scriptures. By the time Monica left for home, Tyson hadn't returned to the office. He texted her twice with scriptures and said he was thinking about her. With a heart of inspiration, she cruised home with praise in her heart.

When it came to dating, Tyson had upped Reggie. For weeks, he enjoyed seeing Monica seven days a week, five at work, dinners or movies on Saturdays, and church on Sundays.

Tracee and Reggie were still doing the once or twice a month visit thing.

Taking advantage of an early warm spring day, Tyson coaxed her to stroll to a nearby restaurant. The nice weather had even enticed children to play in the park.

Despite the lunch crowd at Randell's, the couple was able to snag a table. They placed their orders for salads and sandwiches. While waiting, Tyson linked his fingers through hers and stared. It was a flirtatious game they played to guess what the other was thinking.

He wondered if Monica could see his love reflected in his eyes. Just in case, Tyson couldn't withhold his feelings any longer. "I know it's not the romantic thing to say—"

She squeezed his hand. "Tyson Graham, you've been the most romantic man I've ever met."

He grinned as their orders were delivered to their table. Once they were alone again, he continued, "Even when I want to profess my love over a Caesar salad?"

"You haven't said it yet," she softly challenged and lifted an eyebrow. Her expression was blank, making him wonder if his impatience was a bad move.

Leaning closer, he whispered, "I love you."

Her reaction threw him off. Her eyes watered, her mouth dropped and she patted her chest. Her movements seemed well coordinated as she screamed her excitement, startling him and a few customers at tables close by. She placed her hands on both sides of his jaw and coaxed him closer. "I love you too," she said softly, nibbling on his lips.

Oh no, she wasn't about to outdo him, so Tyson shouted, "Yes," pumping his fist in the air before paying her back with a hard kiss. Beaming with happiness, their appetite wavered and they asked for to-go boxes.

On the stroll back, Tyson took her hand. "Did I tell you how incredibly beautiful you look today?"

"As a matter of fact, you didn't."

Snickering, he scanned her attire: a short powder blue

waist jacket, black pants, which stopped at her ankles, and stacked heels. Yep, she was perfect for him. As a tease, he made an imaginary zipper motion across his mouth.

"Say it," she taunted, tugging on his hands, then she began to walk backward.

He shook his head, holding in his laughter.

"Say it," she repeated, feigning a scowl, which was cute on her.

Voices ahead made Tyson break eye contact. When he spotted some teenagers jumping rope, he concocted his own challenge. He grabbed the love of his life around her waist. She screamed and he teased, "Prove you're the jump rope queen." He pointed to the girls.

"Oh, so you want to talk trash," she said after glancing over her shoulder. "I don't want to interrupt their game."

"It will be worth it." Tyson steered her toward the group. "Excuse me, ladies. My girlfriend here says she can jump rope. I don't believe her. Can you give her a try?"

They looked Monica up and down. "But she has on heels."

"When you start wearing them, you'll be surprised what you can do in them," she advised, slapping her purse against Tyson's chest.

They seemed doubtful, but the tallest girl started to twirl the ropes in both their hands. He folded his arms, watching her body sway with the rhythm. Seconds later, she jumped in and moved with such finesse, she gave him a glimpse of her dominance in high school and college. The girls increased the twirls, and Monica seemed to tap dance effortlessly, then jumped out, ending her performance. Tyson clapped, along with other spectators who had stopped to watch.

With a mischievous glint in her eyes, Monica sashayed up to him, dusting off her hands. "Your turn."

Throwing his head back, he snorted. "I don't think so, Miss Show Off. I can't come close."

Placing a fist on her waist, she tapped her shoe. "I know," she boasted. "Show me what you've got, Graham."

He wasn't a man to back down from a dare. The last time he jumped rope was in college when he boxed for a few years, then he gave it up for football. Yet, he couldn't resist taking the bait. "Hold your purse." He handed over the bag too. "Give me the easy stuff—please," he said to the girls who had been watching their exchange with interest as he stood in the middle and waited.

Giggling, they gave him a single twirl and he jumped, more like hopping from foot to foot. He didn't make it to ten before his shoe got tangled under the rope.

As he lifted his hands up in defeat, he thanked the girls while Monica snapped pictures with her smartphone. He tried to block more shots. "If you show anyone—"

"Relax. I'll only blackmail you when necessary. Besides, a couple of people over there were taping it to upload on YouTube." She giggled.

"I'll always love you." He reassured her, enjoying her playful side.

Slipping her arm through his, she leaned her head on his arm and they finished their walk to the office. "Note to Mr. Graham, the next time you tell me you love me, I want a candlelight dinner."

"Message received." He kissed her hair, looking forward to the weekend for him to do just that.

Chapter Eighteen

"Tyson told me he loved me!" Monica screamed into the phone, waking Veronica from her beauty rest late Saturday night. Having just returned from a romantic dinner with Tyson, she was too keyed up to sleep. This was her perfect life.

"Took him long enough," she stated as if she wasn't surprised, then yawned.

"Actually, he told me yesterday over lunch, but it didn't count until tonight. It was so romantic…"

"Hold your excitement. If you want me to go to church tomorrow with you, then I need all eight hours of my beauty rest."

"Right. Bye, girl." Monica didn't have to be threatened her twice. She had tried for weeks to get her friend to visit, so she wasn't leaving anything to chance.

"Wait," Veronica yelled. "Congratulations, I'm happy for you." *Click*.

To match the warm-and-fuzzy feeling in her heart, Monica strolled into her bedroom and turned on the gas flames in her fireplace. Cuddling up in her robe, she closed her eyes and relived the moments.

Exactly four hours earlier, Tyson had showed up with a

single red rose and a limo parked outside her door. It was a cliché, but so were romance novels and she couldn't get enough of those as a teenager. At his request, she had worn the gown she had on at the ball. He gazed at her with such awe as if it was the first time she had seen her in it.

They dined at a five-star restaurant by candlelight. Reaching across the white linen tablecloth, he held her hands. "At times I've been told I have a habit of not thinking things through, like when I told you I loved you yesterday. I still do today and will tomorrow. I want you to remember that." His eyes sparkled.

Bowing her head, she gathered her thoughts, before meeting his eyes again. "I think our chance meeting on the highway was our road to Damascus. Somehow that chain of events led me to you and Christ. To know you love me despite knowing the worst of me is a special kind of love." She blinked to keep the tears at bay.

"Hey, you act like I don't have faults." He smirked. "I think you've been privy to my judgment calls too."

Their evening was unrushed as they ate and shared dessert. Afterward, they relaxed as the limo driver gave them a tour of their city, which Monica saw very little of. She and Tyson were too busy whispering their words of love.

Reluctantly, their date ended at her door with a short kiss and a long hug. With those memories, she got up, turned off the gas flames, and climbed in bed after saying her prayers of thanks for everything and everyone in her life. Then she surrendered to sweet dreams.

The next day as Veronica had promised, she arrived at church late and had an excuse to leave before Pastor Reed finished his sermon, "Treasures Won't Last Down Here," Matthew 6:19.

Monica didn't hide her disappointment. She wanted her friend to experience firsthand this spiritual strength. They had shared so much in life.

Solae reached over Tyson and whispered comforting

words, "Some people come to Christ willingly. Others come as a last resort. We'll keep praying she comes either way."

"Okay," she mouthed while Tyson squeezed her hand. One thing she had learned over the past weeks was that prayers did change things. Maybe her best friend was next to make a change.

The following Saturday afternoon, she and Tyson attended a matinee at the St. Louis Black Rep. "I think it's time we meet each other's parents," he said casually.

Monica gave him a side glance as they strolled hand in hand back to his SUV. "And you just came up with this idea while you were supposed to be enjoying *Sunset Baby*?"

The tenderness in his eyes made her heart flutter. "When I'm with you, I've learned how to multitask." He paused. "I can profess my love and kiss you at the same time." He beamed before giving her a demonstration.

She giggled, gripping his coat collar. "So are we going to flip a coin to see whose parents we visit first?"

Tyson shook his head. "Nope, my mother and sisters have demanded to meet you since I lost my appetite at the dinner table—well, sort of." Turning her around, he helped her inside his vehicle.

While she buckled up, she couldn't help but wonder how much Tyson told them about her. "Do they know about my attacks?"

He didn't mask the guilt on his face. "I'm sorry, babe," he confessed and her heart sunk.

She hadn't experienced anything in weeks. Prayer was definitely working.

"I discussed it with them when you were first hired. If I knew I was going to fall in love with you, I wouldn't have said anything."

"It's okay." She shrugged. "You couldn't resist me."

His nostrils flared. "You have no idea how right you are."

"So when would you like me to meet them?" She relaxed against the head rest.

"Now."

"Now!!!!" She sprang forward. She couldn't form her thoughts fast enough. "Tyson Graham, you could have prepared me. I could have gotten my hair and nails done, bought a new sweater…"

"Babe, you look perfect without trying, but if it will make you feel any better, they don't know either. It's a surprise for all of you." He grinned and she rolled her eyes.

Men are so clueless, she thought and glanced out the window as he called his mother. She snickered, hearing a piercing scream through Tyson's earpiece.

"Serves you right," she mumbled loud enough for him to hear, and folded her arms. When he disconnected the call, she laughed out loud.

By the time they made it to his parents' home, his sisters had arrived minutes before them and his mother had leftovers warming in the oven. She was amazed how they dropped everything for Tyson.

Despite knowing her secret, the Grahams embraced her without batting an eye and never hinted she wasn't good enough for their brother and son.

When they were ushered to the dining room, the food was blessed and dinner was served. Monica was amused hearing Tyson's childhood stories he hadn't shared with her yet. Before leaving, his younger sister, Gail, pulled her to the side. "Thank you."

"For what?" she asked, perplexed.

"My big brother is stubborn. Once he makes rules, he doesn't break them. But when he met you, something told me you were going to change his heart. We're all convinced true love brought you two together."

"Amen," she whispered as they exchanged goodbye hugs.

"So your parents know nothing about me?" Tyson couldn't believe his ears the following week, watching Monica nod an affirmative from the passenger seat in his SUV. They had been officially dating six weeks. "Should I be hurt or upset by this revelation?" At least his family suspected she would hold a special place in his heart.

Her lips curled into a smile and she squeezed his hand. "Scared? Don't be. My mother knows I've been going out. If she suspected I was dating exclusively, she would hound me about getting married and having children. I didn't want that pressure on our relationship."

Tyson accepted her explanation, but he didn't like it. He figured if everyone at the office knew they were a couple, even the folks at Solae's church, it shouldn't be a secret to Monica's parents.

The Wyatts lived in North County in an older subdivision with well-kept single-story homes. He thought Mrs. Wyatt was going to cry when she answered the door, sniffing, and arms wide open before her daughter even introduced him.

"I can't believe my daughter has been hiding you," she said.

"I can," Mr. Wyatt mumbled, coming up behind his wife. The look in his eyes put Tyson on notice he wasn't easily impressed.

Once their hats and coats were removed, he followed them into a small sitting room off the kitchen. "Mom, there're a lot of things I need to tell you."

"You're pregnant," Mrs. Wyatt stated in horror as they took their seats.

"What!" her father raised his voice as he and Tyson exchanged bewildered glances.

"Ah, no. I told you Tyson and I got our past sins washed away, we're not trying to make any new ones," Monica defended their relationship and he was proud of her.

It was Tyson's idea to tell her parents about the attacks, even if she hadn't suffered any since the day they accepted God's complete salvation.

Her father crossed his arms and leaned back in his seat while her mother scooted to the edge of the sofa.

"I'm starving. Can't we eat first?" Monica practically whined.

"No, let's talk, then we'll feed you," Mr. Wyatt stated.

If Tyson knew they would be interrogated first, he would have insisted they grab a bite earlier, but she refused, stating her mother would be offended they had eaten anything.

"Daddy…"

Doubting her father was going to budge, Tyson squeezed her hand for her to comply.

"Hush, George, I want to hear how they met." Ollie smiled.

She glanced at him again. "A while back, I started having these attacks—"

"What kind of attacks?" Her mother gasped for air, then patted her chest.

"Nothing life-threatening," she hurried to explain.

When Monica seemed concerned at Ollie's reaction, Tyson kept his eyes on her and prayed nobody would be having attacks today on his watch.

"I kinda freaked out for no reason. I felt frightened, started sweating. The next time I was on the highway, another time I was in my car."

"How many times?" her mother asked.

"Four," Tyson answered. "She was having an attack while driving and pulled over to the shoulder. I stopped to see if she was all right." Mr. Wyatt smiled, definitely pleased. "Then I hired her."

"She works for you?" Her father frowned. "I don't like he has the power to fire you."

"Or the power to love her," Tyson stated. "And I do."

"These attacks…" Her mother steered the conversation back to Monica. "You're a very rational and tempered person. For you to act like that out of the blue reminds me of when you were a baby and we caught your Uncle Johnny holding you high in the air, ignoring your pleads to get down, or putting you in the wagon and running fast. The boy was beyond mischievous. After we caught him trying to terrorize you with Halloween masks, your daddy banned him from our house," she explained.

"Uncle Johnny?" Monica said as if she couldn't believe it.

"Yep, Attorney Johnathan Washington Wyatt had a warp sense of humor when he was young." His father *hmph*ed.

"Maybe that had something to do with those fear attacks," her mother reasoned.

"Maybe, but I've never been scared of flying, driving, people…" She shrugged. "So can we eat now?" She feigned starvation. It worked and in less than five minutes, they gathered around the table.

Tyson kept his amusement to himself. His woman had perfected the art of getting her way and better watch himself around the woman he loved her.

Double dating was overrated, judging from the vibes Tyson was getting from Reggie and Tracee. What had happened between last weekend and today?

He and Monica had been excited about joining them for dinner, but the evening was going downhill and fast. She must have sensed the tension too as she tried to engage Tracee. Reggie's girlfriend was polite, giving short answers, but seemed uncomfortable.

What was going on in their paradise? Tyson wondered. The couple definitely wasn't glowing.

"So, Tracee, how long have you and Reggie been dating?"

"Six months and two weeks." Tracee cut her eyes at her boyfriend.

When Reggie excused himself to the men's room, Tyson followed and stopped his friend outside the door. "Hey, man, what's going on?" He tried to keep the edge out of his voice. "The double dating thing was your idea for our ladies to get to know each other, which is what Monica is trying to do. I'd have taken her to a movie or play."

"That was before…" Reggie rubbed his neck and glanced away. Finally, he looked Tyson in the eyes. "I hate to say you were right, man, but the long-distance relationship is wearing us down. Changes need to be made. She ain't moving and neither am I, so there you have it. The handwriting is on the wall." He made quotation marks with his fingers.

"The double date was planned before Tracee decided, without my input, that we should go our separate ways. She felt I deserved to be told face-to-face." Reggie twisted his mouth. He looked wounded. "She told me she was going to wait until after dinner, but it was too much to hold in." He pointed back at the table. "You can blame her for ruining the night."

Tyson had never seen his business partner so discombobulated. Neither had he seen him so enthralled with a woman. "Man, I'm sorry." He glanced back. Tracee seemed to have no problem talking in their absence.

Two more names would be added to Tyson's prayer list, because his heart ached for Reggie. "Listen…after we eat, let's call it a night. Clearly, you and Tracee's hearts aren't in this and I want to salvage the night with Monica."

"Fine with me. If this wasn't an upscale restaurant, we could order to-go meals," Reggie sputtered and walked into the men's room.

Tyson didn't follow this time. Instead he whispered a short prayer, "Lord, what can I do or say? Reggie's hurting."

Pray My will, God whispered back.

Chapter Nineteen

"This will be our first weekend apart," Tyson told Monica as he packed for a business conference in Florida, the same one where Reggie had met Tracee. It was an unspoken rule after he and Tracee started dating that only Reggie would go on that trip.

That was before their relationship ended. Now, his business partner balked at any mention of Florida. Tyson had to rearrange his schedule for this trip. This was bad timing as they both were focused on drawing new clients and submitting some of their best campaigns for the Marcom Awards.

"I'll miss you." Her voice was soft. "Do you plan to reach out to Tracee while you're in Tampa?"

"Nope," he answered with little thought. "If they're going to kiss and make up, they won't need my intervention. If we had a disagreement, I would want us to kiss" —he lowered his voice— "and make up."

"Me too. I don't want to play games."

"See, and that's why I don't want to get in the middle of it. I'm going to sit in on two workshops and come back home to my woman." He hadn't zipped up his garment bag and he missed her already.

"Be safe."

"You too, babe." After a series of kisses, and a short prayer, they reluctantly said their 'I love you's and goodbyes.'

Monday started off as a typical day for Monica. After meeting Veronica for dinner and a brief shopping binge, normalcy got lost on her way home from the mall.

"It can't be." She refused to accept the eerie feeling creeping over her shoulders as if it was coming from the back seat. Her hands began to sweat and her heart raced. Was this her appointed time to die while Tyson was so far away? She voice activated a call to him. Her breathing was shallow. She couldn't pass out yet, not until she reached him.

Getting his voicemail, she blinked away a tear and whimpered, "Jesus, You healed me. Why is this happening to me?"

The attack seemed greater than the last one on the night Tyson followed her. She could make the less than five miles home. "Come on." She pounded the wheel, debating whether to pull off on the shoulder and wait for this episode to pass, or defy death and keep driving.

Your life is in my hands, God whispered.

What does that mean? Was she going to live or die? Immediately, her headset alerted her to a call seconds before the ringtone identified the caller. "Tyson, I'm scared." Her voice cracked when she answered.

"Baby, what's wrong?" The alarm in his voice sounded as raw as her fear.

"I'm having an attack—I guess. How is that possible? Didn't God heal me?"

"*Shh*, it's going to be okay. Where are you?"

"On I-170, leaving the Galleria. I met Veronica—"

"She's not with you?" He let out a frustrated sigh. "Okay, listen to me. I love you. I want you to keep both hands on the wheel and drive while I pray you home."

She nodded, gripping the wheel tighter as cars zoomed past her thirty-mile-an-hour cruise in the slow lane. Some honked, startling her and causing her body to shake. She began to feel faint. She didn't want to die without seeing Tyson one last time. "I love you. If anything happens—"

Tyson drowned her out. "Father, in the mighty name of Jesus, You see all things and know all things. Monica needs to know You're in the car with her. Remind her she belongs to You, not the devil. You didn't give her a spirit of fear, but a sound mind. Satan, I rebuke you in the name of Jesus. You had to get permission from God to taunt her, but the Bible says demons tremor at the name of Jesus. You heard me! Release your hold in the name of Jesus…"

The more he prayed, Monica accelerated until the Olive Street Road exit came into view. *Stay focused*, she kept telling herself as Tyson petitioned the Lord on her behalf until suddenly God took control of his tongues and spoke in a heavenly language. There was no interpretation, but fear immediately left her as she felt God's presence.

By the time she exited off the highway, God's anointing had touched her spirit. While stopped at the first red light, she began to worship Him, drawing attention from the motorist on her left. When the light flashed green, the driver peeled rubber, leaping into the intersection to apparently get away from her.

When she turned into her complex's parking lot minutes later, she collapsed over her wheel, exhausted from the anguish but relieved to see her front door. "I'm home."

Tyson sang a worship song of thanks. She blended her off-key voice with his until they faded to silence. After grabbing her purse and bag, she stepped out of the car, but Tyson refused to disconnect. "I don't know what happened," she tried to explain, but thinking about it brought fresh tears.

"*Shh.* What's Veronica's number?"

"Huh? Why?" Monica frowned as she unlocked the door and walked inside. There was no sense in arguing with him. She was too drained anyway, so she caved in.

She paced the floor in her bedroom as she undressed. She couldn't stand still. "Lord, did You forsake me? Why did that happen?" Her barrage of questions led her to her Bible. The more she read, the calmer her spirit became. She was reading 2 Timothy 1 when her doorbell rang, followed by fanatic knocking. Next, she heard Veronica's voice. "Open up, Monica."

When she did, her friend nearly knocked her over, getting inside. "Tyson called and asked me to spend the night. He sounded alarmed, which of course freaked me out, because I thought God healed you…" she rambled as she dumped an overnight bag on the floor.

"Wait a minute. You're spending the night? On a work night?"

"Yep." She removed her coat, then looped her arm through hers. "Come on. Make me some coffee and you can tell me what happened when we left each other."

For the first time since leaving the Galleria, she saw something funny. "I thought you came to comfort me."

"I did and it starts with a cup of your half coffee, half hot chocolate combo." She pulled out her cell phone and tapped in numbers. "Ty, this is Ronnie…"

Ty and Ronnie? Monica repeated in her head. When did they become so chummy? Her friend never used her childhood nickname…and Ty? She smirked, watching her friend nod and laugh. Glad for the company, Monica was about to step into the kitchen to prepare her drink request when Veronica snapped pictures of her, then texted them to Tyson.

"Here, your man wants to talk to you." She handed over the phone.

"Thank you," she whispered softly. "I don't know what you said to Veronica to convince her to come on a work night and this late…"

"I'll would move mountains to take care of you. But we're going to keep praying and believing God will move this mountain."

Closing her eyes, she allowed each word to seep into her heart. "Saying I love you back doesn't seem like it's enough."

He chuckled. "Believe me, Miss Wyatt, it is."

Opening her eyes, she glanced back in the kitchen. Veronica was making her own coffee concoction. Grinning, her friend lifted her mug up in a mock cheers. "Your brother ain't got nothing on Ty. I want me one of them."

"Then come to church and stay for the entire service," she mouthed. "As you can imagine, I'm drained and it's getting late. Veronica and I both have to get up for work—"

"Nope, Ronnie agreed…"

Ronnie again? God had truly blessed her with a good friend and a good man.

"…to take a day off, so I want you to work from home tomorrow. That is not up for discussion. I'll call Reggie and advise him."

"So, you're pulling employer-employee rank on me?" She could feel her defiance rising.

"No, baby. This is a plea from a man who loves you and regrets not being there to put his arms around you to kiss and pray to make it better. Veronica was the best I could do."

Monica laughed, and so did Tyson before they disconnected. She would never admit it, but she was glad she had a day to recover. She strolled back in the kitchen, poured her brew into a mug, blessed it in Jesus's name, and took a sip. Eying Veronica, Monica giggled. "So you went back thirty years to Ronnie? And Ty?"

"Hey." She shrugged. "Your man cares about you. He's good peeps. I wanted him to know he can count on me. Plus, I owed him for that sub sandwich he brought me when I was sick."

"Whatever, Ronnie," she teased.

"Now, from the beginning, what happened between us driving off the parking lot and you getting home?"

Once Monica recapped, Veronica asked, "Isn't that what your salvation was all about, getting healed and stuff?"

"I know Jesus healed my soul." Monica didn't say more, because she was confused.

Veronica *hmm*ed. She rested her cup on a coaster and leaned forward. "Maybe God is going to use the doctors to heal you. Your ninetieth day is almost here. You have no excuse for not getting evaluated and put on medication. Trust me, you're going to give Tyson gray hair before he marries you."

"Marries me?" She fumbled with her hands. "Tonight may give him enough reason not to ask me."

"God's going to get you for lying. Ty has been praying for you since day one, and he doesn't seem like a man to back down." She yawned. "I need my eight hours, starting now. I assume my guest room is ready? Good night." Veronica stood, gathered her tote, and walked down the hall to the other bedroom.

Monica reached for her Bible. The devil was a liar. She trusted God to heal her body and soul.

According to My will, He whispered.

Chapter Twenty

Tyson was hot! The devil was a coward to wait until he was gone to wreak havoc on his woman.

Tuesday morning, he prayed longer than usual and read as many chapters as he could find in his Bible on spiritual warfare. He called Monica after he showered and dressed. "How did you sleep?"

"Great, actually. I went to bed with Jesus and woke up with Him. Reading His Word was comforting. Now, I'm cooking Ronnie" —she giggled— "and me some omelets."

Tyson grunted. "I sent her over there to take care of you."

"Yeah, well, this is one of the casualties of Veronica doing favors. It always costs me in the kitchen."

"Hey, I heard that!" she said in the background. "Good morning, Ty."

He chuckled and returned her greeting through Monica. They chatted a few more minutes, then disconnected.

Before checking out of the hotel, Tyson made two more calls. First to Reggie to let him know he asked Monica to work from home.

"Is she okay?"

"Yes, she is now. I'll go check on her as soon as my plane lands."

"I would do the same for Trac—that's over." He paused. "Have you seen her?"

"I haven't." Tyson didn't say more. He didn't offer to reach out either. He had his own woman to focus on.

"Okay. Well, be safe, learn a lot, and I guess I'll see you two tomorrow."

"Yep." Next he called Solae and didn't waste time explaining what had happened. "I know Tuesdays and Thursdays are your off days, but do you mind going to visit and pray for her? Her friend stayed the night, but she needs a spiritual sister right now."

"You don't have to ask twice. I'm on it."

"Thank you." His day just got better.

"I want me a Tyson Graham." Veronica pouted, carrying a vase of flowers into Monica's bedroom.

She hadn't heard the doorbell ring as she focused on research for a prospective client. "Sorry." She took the flowers. "He's taken." Setting them on the table near her bay window, she took the card and read it: *You're my everything.* Minutes later, the doorbell rang again. Secretly hoping it was Tyson, she beat Veronica to answer it. She screamed her delight at seeing Solae. "What are you doing here?"

"Tyson called me this morning, so here I am." She smiled.

"Yeah, well get in line. He called me last night," Veronica joked and waved.

"So what happened?" Solae frowned and removed her coat, then scanned her interior. "This is nice."

"I decorated it." Veronica raised her hand again.

"She can show you around," she explained, pointing to Veronica, "but let me finish running numbers and I'll tell you all about it."

Not even an hour later, Monica walked out of her bedroom to see her friends laughing hysterically at a comedy sitcom. Urging Solae into the kitchen, Monica confessed her doubts once they were seated at the table. "I really thought God had healed me when I got baptized. When I resurfaced from the water, I felt so light, surely every sickness was gone. Although I knew salvation was about my soul."

"Did God tell you He was going to heal you?" Solae asked.

Shaking her head, Monica answered no. "I just assumed."

"Her insurance kicks in soon," Veronica yelled over her shoulder, eavesdropping. "I told her God can heal her through the doctors."

"Physicians practice medicine to bring about healing. God is the Healer and doesn't need any practice. The Bible says if any be sick among you, let them call for the elders of the church to lay hands and pray."

"I can do that, so you think I should wait on God and not go to the doctor?"

Solae lifted both hands. "I didn't say that. I think you need to get prayer from one of the elders at church. I also think you need to go to the doctor and get an official diagnosis." She paused.

"When I was in my twenties, I suffered from agonizing menstrual periods along with severe migraines. I was already saved and got prayer before I went to doctors, trying to get relief from both ailments. Finally, one doctor put me on the strongest medicine for my migraines, but nothing could keep them at bay. I was nauseated, had to stay home from work, had blurred vision—the works, but I still took the medicine. One day while driving and my mind was elsewhere, I heard God speak, 'I'm going to heal you and you won't know when I've done it.'"

She had heard God too, but He didn't mention anything about her healing.

"Well, as a chronic migraine sufferer, my few migraines became less frequent until I realized they no longer accompanied my menstrual cramping and heavy bleeding. The doctors took care of my heavy bleeding with a total abdominal hysterectomy and Jesus took care of my migraines by speaking it."

"Wow," Veronica said, walking into the kitchen. "I thought once Monica was saved, everything would be all right."

Solae cited a couple of scriptures. "As long as we live in this world, the devil will come at us. His days are numbered and God will either heal our friend or equip Monica with spiritual warfare to resist the devil's tactics."

Veronica seemed to be engaged, asking questions until Solae checked the time. "I've got to pick up my children from school, so let's pray." Before she left, she snapped a selfie. "Orders from your man."

"Of course." Everyone laughed and hugged Solae goodbye.

Veronica went back to watching movies and Monica finished up work, then she warmed up leftovers for dinner. After they ate, Veronica cleaned the kitchen. "My assignment here is done. I'm heading home." They hugged each other. "I'm glad you have Tyson and Solae. You can't go wrong with them two."

"But you will always be my number one sister-girlfriend."

After Veronica left, Monica waited for Tyson's plane to land in St. Louis. When it did, he texted: I know it's late, but I'm stopping by.

When her doorbell rang, she opened it. Although Tyson looked worn out and stressed, he rushed in, wrapped his arms around her, and lifted her off her feet. He smothered her with kisses before setting her down, but he didn't let her go.

Stepping back, he scrutinized her as if he was looking for battle scars. Seemingly satisfied she was okay, he kissed her again. "I'll pick you up for work tomorrow. Good night."

Monica blinked at the whirlwind moment. She was so glad it wasn't a dream.

Chapter Twenty-One

The elders at Rapture Ready Church laid hands on Monica and prayed for her deliverance. Tyson was at her side. Four days after her insurance kicked in, he accompanied her to the doctor.

Because of her symptoms, she was diagnosed with an anxiety disorder and not generalized anxiety that everyone experiences from time to time. "Miss Wyatt, more than forty million Americans suffer with one form or another anxiety, but this is treatable." He prescribed medications, and suggested a follow-up in a month.

She was disappointed, but thanked him. "He confirmed my fears."

Tyson squeezed her hand as they left the doctor's office. "Babe, I don't know a lot of scriptures, but I have to believe prayer means something or He wouldn't tell us to pray without ceasing."

Monica sighed. "Yeah."

Ironically, after she began to take the medicine, God spoke. *I'm going to heal you.*

"*Why* did You wait until now to say something? When, Lord?"

She didn't wait for His answer as she was about to defy

her doctor and stop the medicine cold turkey, but Dr. Davis strongly advised her against that.

"God will let you know when this trial is over." Solae had convinced her at work.

Tyson reasoned with her as he continued to fast and pray. She admitted she did feel calmer with the drug, but was concerned about possible side effects. "I don't want to gain weight, get addicted, or become suicidal," she murmured, despite enjoying a picnic at the park near their company.

"Baby, your enchanting eyes are your best asset. If you pick up weight, you'll still belong to me. Don't women pick up weight after they have a baby? And we have to discuss how many we want." He took a sip from one of the plastic champagne glasses he had filled with sparkling grape juice. He had gone all out for an hour lunch.

"Plus, God said He was going to heal you, which means it will come to pass. As Solae says, 'We have to impress God with our faith no matter what devices the devil throws at us—'"

"Hold up." She frowned. "Let's backtrack to the weight gain part from the medicine and the babies…" She lifted an eyebrow. "How can you talk about babies when you haven't proposed?"

He bobbed his head. "You're right." He rested his glass in the basket and took hers and did the same. Her heart pounded at the unknown.

Taking both her hands, Tyson stood and pulled her to her feet. He rubbed her hands and gazed into her eyes. "I can't think of another woman…" he knelt, "…who I would want to spend my life with, have my babies, and be my prayer partner, so…will you marry me?"

"Yes."

He leaped up, lifted her off her feet, and spun her around before steadying her. She laughed as he fumbled with the ring box in his pocket, then opened it.

The sunrays' brilliance touched the diamond, causing it to sparkle as he slipped it on her finger. "It's beautiful." She kissed him, then stepped back, folded her arms, and feigned insult. "I know you've got something more special than our lunch hour to propose to me."

"But of course, Miss Wyatt."

Surprisingly, they didn't return to the office. "Let's go for a ride," he suggested a little too mysteriously.

"Where are we going?"

She soon found out when she spied three Tyson & Dyson Communications billboards with his proposals: one, he was on his knees with a puppy dog expression; the second billboard showed her ring; and the third was a picture of them with a caption: *She said yes!*

Monica was speechless. She faced him. The money they forfeited to run the proposal was costing the company. She stroked his chin. "You have outdone yourself."

"Then you like it?"

"Yes, but what if I had said no?"

"It would have stayed up there until you caved in. For now, just the weekend."

After that excursion, they played hooky from work to go home and get ready for an evening of celebration, beginning with telling their parents.

Chapter Twenty-Two

Four months later...

This was it. In less than an hour, Monica Wyatt would become Mrs. Tyson Graham. She exhaled slowly as she left the bride's chamber on her father's arm. More than anything, she prayed they would have a long happy life ahead and she would give him beautiful or handsome babies.

Over the years, her resolutions had come and gone, but this year, the best resolution had been for her and Veronica to go back to church. Her eyes glazed as the double doors opened to a dimly lit sanctuary for the candlelight ceremony. She swallowed as guests stood.

As she glided down the aisle toward the man God sent her way, Monica admired his stance: straight and confident. His handsomeness seemed to be engulfed in a cocoon of contentment. Marrying him felt right as his eyes pulled her in and dared her not to look away. In her peripheral vision, people's heads turned back and forth from her to Tyson. Reggie, the best man, stood next to him and her brother, who had returned from his tour, was one of two groomsmen.

Pausing at the assigned place in the aisle, she waited as Tyson's long strides came her way until he towered over her.

She could see the fire in his eyes as his nostrils flared. As if remembering her father, he quickly diverted his attention from her long enough for a handshake.

"Love her," her father demanded.

"Always, sir," he answered.

Releasing his hold, her father kissed her cheek and stepped back to allow Tyson to guide her to the altar.

"Dearly, beloved, we are gathered here today…" Pastor Reed began.

As they repeated their vows, she stared into Tyson's eyes. She saw the promise of his love as he professed each word.

"Monica, I will honor you, protect, and pray for you until the Lord takes my last breath. I love you."

With teary eyes, she said her vows, then she exhaled. Although she was a little unsure of the future, she had faith and trusted this man with her heart, body, and now soul. She was in good hands.

"By the power of God invested in me and the state of Missouri, I now pronounce you Mr. and Mrs. Tyson Graham. What the Lord has joined together from the beginning of time, let no demon, whether in the form of a handsome man or an alluring woman, come between and destroy what God has given you. In Jesus's name. Amen. You may now salute Mrs. Graham."

Monica shivered when she heard herself addressed as Mrs., but her groom seemed either to be in no rush to seal the deal, or everything was moving in slow motion.

The smirk on his lips answered her question. He would not be rushed as he lifted the veil and lovingly gathered her in his arms. Closing her eyes, she waited impatiently for the kiss. When it arrived, it was like no other they had shared. It was of possession, leaving no doubt she belonged to him and she returned the assault, reminding him that he now belonged to her.

Author's Note:

I hope you've enjoyed Monica and Tyson's story. Please tell others and post a review on Amazon and Goodreads. I would appreciate it!

While researching this story, I watched some very cool digital billboards on YouTube. I hope to revisit this fascinating industry, because the novella didn't allow me enough space to explore it to the extent I wanted. In the meanwhile, visit YouTube and plug in these titles in the search box and enjoy.

British Airways Clever Billboard Incorporates Real Flights
The Most Creative Billboard Ads
The billboard that produces potable water out of air

If you've read my work before, then you know I like to put a little of myself into the stories. *Every Woman Needs A Praying Man* is no exception. God is mighty and He has performed mighty works in my life. Years ago, I did suffer from severe, disabling migraine headaches where my vision blurred, and I was allergic to two migraine medicines.

God spoke to me exactly as I had Him in the scene with Solae. Let my testimony serve as a reminder that God is still performing miracles.

Want to know about my next release? Sign up for my monthly newsletter at www.patsimmons.net

Be blessed!

Book Discussion Questions:

- Can you name a few scriptures that deal with spiritual warfare?
- Discuss Tyson 's attitude when he visited the church to get prayer for Monica only and not himself.
- What is a panic attack?
- Is medication always needed?
- If someone close to you experienced a panic attack, how did you respond?
- Describe Tyson 's character—too hard on Monica or reasonable, considering he didn't know what was going on with her.
- What do you think triggered Monica 's panic attacks?
- Have you ever been healed of a condition without asking for it?
- Has God healed you of anything you want to share?

About the Author

Pat Simmons is a self-proclaimed genealogy sleuth who is passionate about researching her ancestors and then casting them in starring roles in her novels, in the hope of tracking down any distant relatives who might happen to pick up her books. She has been a genealogy enthusiast since her great-grandmother, Minerva Brown Wade, died at the age of ninety-seven in 1988.

Pat describes the evidence of the gift of the Holy Ghost as an amazing, unforgettable, life-altering experience. She believes God is the Author who advances the stories she writes.

Pat holds a B.S. in Mass Communications from Emerson College in Boston, Massachusetts. She has worked in various positions in radio, television, and print media for more than twenty years. Currently, she oversees the media publicity for the annual RT Booklovers Conventions.

She is the multi-published author of thirty single titles and eBook novellas, including the #1 Amazon bestseller in God's Word category, *A Christian Christmas*. Her award-winning titles include *Talk to Me*, ranked #14 of Top Books in 2008 that Changed Lives by *Black Pearls Magazine*. She is a two-time recipient of the Romance Slam Jam Emma Rodgers Award for Best Inspirational Romance for *Still Guilty* (2010) and

Crowning Glory (2011). Her beloved Jamieson men are featured in the *Guilty* series: *Guilty of Love*, *Not Guilty of Love*, *Still Guilty*, and *The Acquittal*; the Jamieson Legacy series continues in *Guilty by Association*, *The Guilt Trip*, *Free from Guilt* and *The Confession* (nominated for Best Inspirational Romance).

Pat introduced the Carmen Sisters series in *No Easy Catch*, *In Defense of Love*, *Driven to Be Loved* (National Bestseller) and *Redeeming Heart*.

In addition to researching her roots and sewing, she has been a featured speaker and workshop presenter at various venues across the country.

Pat has converted her sofa-strapped sports fanatic husband into an amateur travel agent, untrained bodyguard, GPS-guided chauffeur, and administrative assistant who is constantly on probation. They have a son and a daughter.

Readers may learn more about Pat and her books by visiting her Web site, www.patsimmons.net; connecting with her on Twitter, Facebook, Pinterest, or LinkedIn or by contacting her at authorpatsimmons@gmail.com.

Excerpt from
THE CONFESSION

Chapter One

"Excuse me." The richness of a baritone voice interrupted Sandra Nicholson's next sip of java as she stared out the window at the Nook Café. Glancing over her shoulder, Sandra expected to see… Well, she didn't know what she expected, but the good-looking gentleman with defined features wasn't it.

The mesmerizing voice matched a captivating man. *Wow*, she thought to herself as he seemed to study her.

"You are one incredibly beautiful woman," he stated as he towered over the table she shared with her son, who had minutes earlier excused himself to the men's room.

The stranger's timing couldn't have been more precise. A snarl from her overbearing son, and the man surely would have thought twice about stopping. What was taking Kidd so long, anyway?

Without waiting for her response, the distinguished gentleman swaggered out of Nordstrom's boutique café and disappeared into the store, leaving a trail of his designer cologne as his calling card. His stride had been as confident as his declaration.

Sandra did her best not to ogle, but she conducted a quick assessment in less than sixty seconds. She guessed him to be about six-one or two and would tower over her five-seven frame. Judging from his wavy thick salt-and-pepper curly hair that complemented his brown skin, the man was in his late forties, early fifties. If good genes ran in his family, he could have been hovering over eighty for all she knew. Yet, his confident stride hinted of a man who was youthful and fit. With jaw-dropping looks, she pegged him as a ladies man in his heyday, or even now. Sandra knew how to call them, because she had been charmed by the top-of-the-line Samuel Jamieson. She dismissed the temptation at the same time Kidd reappeared, talking on his cell phone.

"Eva," he mouthed.

She nodded as he took his seat, then her mind drifted once again to the striking stranger. It wasn't like she didn't receive compliments here and there, but it was the commanding way he said it that made her want to pass out and never regain consciousness if it meant he would be in her dreams. Because he said it, Sandra felt beautiful. Maybe it was the highlights in her hair that her daughter-in-law, Talise, insisted she try or maybe it was the ensemble she had meticulously assembled to wear.

"Okay, babe. Don't worry. I'm on my way." Lines etched Kidd's forehead, which put Sandra on alert. No time for whimsical musing as she leaned forward with concern. "Is everything okay?"

"No." He gritted his teeth. "The car won't start and Kennedy has a doctor's appointment. Sorry, Mom, we have to cut our breakfast date short." He stood and pulled a twenty out his wallet then kissed her cheek. "Are you going to be all right?"

Sandra smiled. "No apologies needed, son. Go see about my grandbaby. She's your priority."

"But you're right up there at the top of my list too." Snatching his jacket off the back of his chair, he hurried off.

The monthly breakfast treat was her older son's idea for some one-on-one time. Even though he was married, he still felt obligated to look after her as if she was an ailing out-of-shape granny in her eighties, not a woman who had yet to experience a hot flash.

In her mid-50s, Sandra had regrets in her life. One, she had yet to marry. Even after she repented of her deeds and accepted the salvation outlined in the Book of Acts, God hadn't blessed her in that way. Second, the man who fathered her two sons out of wedlock wasn't worth the heartache he caused her. But the Lord had given her two beautiful granddaughters to spoil—one from each son. And she did without any guilt trips from their scolding.

As a personal fashion consultant and shopper, Sandra set her own schedule. She didn't have to meet with her client until this afternoon. She had worked in the insurance industry for most of her adult life to provide for her boys. With her 401K and pension, Sandra had quit her job in Boston and relocated to St. Louis to be closer to family. That move seemed to liberate her and she explored her creative side. She was finally, after thirty years, putting her fashion merchandising degree to work.

Sandra glanced around the café. No other male patron seemed to pay her any mind. She didn't consider herself vain. She strived to live with a humble spirit, but a male compliment, not coming from her sons, did make her smile. *Wait until I tell the Jamieson girls about this.* She chuckled as she finished her crepes and fruit.

I can't believe what I just said. Raimond Mayfield snickered, amused by his actions, but he had no regrets. He had told the truth.

It was as if God was his dining partner and had turned his head in the direction of that beautiful woman. But his womanizing days were long gone and God had his record when he repented of his past sins.

Yet, the Lord seemed to push him out of his seat, because he wasn't moving fast enough. Once Raimond began his trek, there was no turning back.

Somehow Raimond managed to sneak a peek at her hands. All fingers were void of jewelry. Her beauty so empowered him that he briefly thought about inviting himself to join her. But he saw another plate and her dining companion was missing, so he decided to keep going. In hindsight, he should have stuck around and introduced himself, if for no other reason, on a professional level as curator of the new Black museum.

He walked aimlessly through the men's clothing section, but his mind was still in the café. Raimond couldn't shake the natural glow from her face when she turned around. His eyes seemed to zoom in on her features like a microscope. The small curve of her cheeks seemed to be positioned to be cupped by a man's hands. Her hair framed her face and her brown eyes brightened when they met his. Her lips puckered, but nothing came out. Yes, God had formed a masterpiece.

Raimond was no stranger to beauties; he had married one. Later, they divorced, to no fault of his ex-wife, but his. Then for years, Raimond enjoyed the endless selection in the dating pool.

That was, until Jesus commandeered his soul and he had repented shamefully before he was baptized with water and fire in Jesus' name. God had truly become his heart regulator.

So what happened back there? Raimond had just concluded an early morning business meeting with a senior manager in one of the departments at Nordstrom. The potential backer's interest was piqued by Raimond's theme for The Heritage House. His mind switched back to his sweet tooth, in the form of a woman and not a pastry on the shelf.

Raimond felt like a giddy teenager rather than a seasoned

adult. Banishing all thoughts of the woman, he browsed through the shirts selection. "Lord, why did You have me make a fool out of myself?" he mumbled as he grabbed three shirts then stepped over the rack of ties.

Suddenly, he experienced an unexplainable sensation that ran down his back. Then the soft melodious female voice spoke from behind him.

"Pick the lilac shirt and that yellow and lilac print tie." The same beautiful woman came to his side. He was speechless as her lips puckered, as if she was contemplating his purchase as her own. "Get the lilac and yellow paisley. It goes good with your skin tone."

With the wave of her hand, she strutted away in a dress that outlined her figure, and all Raimond could do was stare with his jaw slacked. *God, did You do that?*

Once he closed his mouth and breathed, Raimond acted like an obedient student. He checked the shirt's neck size and grabbed the tie the beauty queen had suggested, then he sought out a clerk to ring his purchase.

Twice their paths had crossed—two times, he repeated looking at his fingers. He didn't believe in coincidences. "Lord, if You give me one more chance today, I'll take it as a sign to properly introduce myself and get her number." Next time, *if* there was a next time, Raimond wouldn't be tongue-tied again.

The clerk greeted him and accepted his merchandise. After verifying the sale price and changing the register tape, the transaction was complete. The young man handed Raimond the bag with a smile. "Thanks for shopping at Nordstrom. Enjoy your day."

Not without seeing that woman again, I won't, Raimond thought. He trekked to the women's department, then the perfume counters, but there was no sign of the lady in orange, peach, or whatever the shade she was wearing. He huffed and did another sweep of the store, which wasn't crowded. *Gone.*

Heading to the parking lot, Raimond chalked it up to a

missed opportunity. He strolled to his SUV, tossed his purchases in the back, and slid behind the wheel. While waiting at the light to exit the shopping plaza, he lowered his window to enjoy the freshness of spring. A flash of orange came into his peripheral vision at the same time the light changed to green, and he accelerated. He whipped his head around—it was "her."

He lost all manner of proper etiquette as he honked and yelled, "Excuse me, excuse me." He waved to get her attention. That's when Raimond slammed into the back of the car in front of him.

End of excerpt. Pick up the story by downloading your copy of THE CONFESSION today.

Other Christian titles include:

The Guilty series
Book I: *Guilty of Love*
Book II: *Not Guilty of Love*
Book III: *Still Guilty*
Book IV: *The Acquittal*

The Jamieson Legacy
Book V: *Guilty by Association*
Book VI: *The Guilt Trip*
Book VII: *Free from Guilt*
Sandra Nicholson: Backstory to The Confession
Book VIII: *The Confession*

The Carmen Sisters
Book I: *No Easy Catch*
Book II: *In Defense of Love*
Book III: *Driven to Be Loved*
Book IV: *Redeeming Heart*

Love at the Crossroads
Book I: *Stopping Traffic*
Book II: *A Baby for Christmas*
Book III: *The Keepsake*
Book IV: *What God Has for Me*
Book V: *Every Woman Needs A Praying Man*

Making Love Work Anthology
Book I: *Love at Work*
Book II: *Words of Love*
Book III: *A Mother's Love*

Single titles
Crowning Glory
Jet: Back Story to Led by the Spirit
Love Led by the Spirit
Talk to Me
Her Dress (novella)

Holiday titles

Love for the Holidays (Three Christian novellas)
A Christian Christmas (Book 1 Andersen Brothers)
A Christian Easter
A Christian Father's Day
A Woman After David's Heart (Valentine's Day) (Book 2 Andersen Brothers)
Christmas Greetings
A Noelle for Nathan (Book 3 Andersen Brothers)

LOVE AT THE CROSSROADS SERIES

Stopping Traffic, Book I. Candace Clark has a phobia about crossing the street, and for good reason. As fate would have it, her daughter's principal assigns her to crossing guard duties as part of the school's Parent Participation program. With no choice in the matter, Candace begrudgingly accepts her stop sign and safety vest, and then reports to her designated crosswalk. Once Candace is determined to overcome her fears, God opens the door for a blessing, and Royce Kavanaugh enters into her life, a firefighter built to rescue any damsel in distress. When a spark of attraction ignites, Candace and Royce soon discover there's more than one way to stop traffic.

A Baby For Christmas, Book II. Yes, diamonds are a girl's best friend, but in Solae Wyatt-Palmer's case, she desires something more valuable. Captain Hershel Kavanaugh is a divorcee and the father of two adorable little boys. Solae has never been married and longs to be a mother. Although Hershel showers her with expensive gifts, his hesitation about proposing causes Solae to walk and never look back. As the holidays approach, Hershel must convince Solae that she has everything he could ever want for Christmas.

The Keepsake, Book III. Until death us do part…or until Desiree walks away. Desiree "Desi" Bishop is devastated when she finds evidence of her husband's affair. God knew she didn't get married only to one day have to stand before a judge and file for a divorce. But Desi wants out no matter how much her heart says to forgive Michael. That isn't easier said than done. She sees God's one acceptable reason for a divorce as the only opt-out clause in her marriage. Michael Bishop is a repenting man who loves his wife of three years. If only…he had paid attention to the red flags God sent to keep him from falling into the devil's snares. But Michael didn't and he had fallen. Although God had forgiven him instantly when he repented, Desi's forgiveness is moving as a snail's pace. In the end, after all the tears have been shed and forgiveness granted and received, the couple learns that some marriages are worth keeping.

What God Has For Me, Book IV. Halcyon Holland is leaving her live-in boyfriend, taking their daughter and the baby in her belly with her. She's tired of waiting for the ring, so she buys herself one. When her ex doesn't reconcile their relationship, Halcyon begins to second-guess whether or not she compromised her chance for a happily ever after. After all, what man in his right mind would want to deal with the community stigma of 'baby mama drama?' But Zachary Bishop has had his eye on Halcyon since the first time he saw her. Without a ring on her finger, Zachary prays that she will come to her senses and not only leave Scott, but come back to God. What one man doesn't cherish, Zach is ready to treasure. Not deterred by Halcyon's broken spirit, Zachary is on a mission to offer her a second chance at love that she can't refuse. And as far as her adorable children are concerned, Zachary's love is unconditional for a ready-made family. Halcyon will soon learn that her past circumstances won't hinder the Lord's blessings, because what God has for her, is for her…and him…and the children.

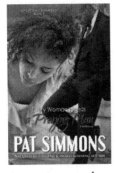

Every Woman Needs A Praying Man, Book V. First impressions can make or break a business deal and it definitely could be a relationship buster, but the ill-timing of a panic attack draws two strangers together. Unlike firefighters who run into danger, instincts tell businessman Tyson Graham to head the other way as fast as he can when he meets a certain damsel in distress. Days later, the same woman struts through his door for a job interview. Monica Wyatt might possess the outwardly beauty and the brains on paper, but Tyson doesn't trust her to work for his firm, or maybe he doesn't trust his heart around her.

LOVE FOR THE HOLIDAYS SERIES

A Christian Christmas. Christian's Christmas will never be the same for Joy Knight if Christian Andersen has his way. Not to be confused with a secret Santa, Christian and his family are busier than Santa's elves making sure the Lord's blessings are distributed to those less fortunate by Christmas day. Joy is playing the hand that life dealt her, rearing four children in a home that is on the brink of foreclosure. She's not looking for a handout, but when Christian rescues her in the checkout line; her niece thinks Christian is an angel. Joy thinks he's just another man who will eventually leave, disappointing her and the children. Although Christian is a servant of the Lord, he is a flesh and blood man and all he wants for Christmas is Joy Knight. Can time spent with Christian turn Joy's attention from her financial woes to the real meaning of Christmas—and true love?

A Christian Easter. How to celebrate Easter becomes a balancing act for Christian and Joy Andersen and their four children. Chocolate bunnies, colorful stuffed baskets and flashy fashion shows are their competition. Despite the enticements, Christian refuses to succumb without a fight. And it becomes a tug of war when his recently adopted ten year-old daughter, Bethani, wants to participate in her friend's Easter tradition. Christian hopes he has instilled Proverbs 22:6, into the children's heart in the short time of being their dad.

A Christian Father's Day. Three fathers, one Father's Day and four children. Will the real dad, please stand up. It's never too late to be a father—or is it? Christian Andersen was looking forward to spending his first Father's day with his adopted children---all four of them. But Father's day becomes more complicated than Christian or Joy ever imagined. Christian finds himself faced with living up to his name when things don't go his way to enjoy an idyllic once a year celebration. But he depends on God to guide him through the journey.

A Woman After David's Heart. David Andersen doesn't have a problem indulging in Valentine's Day, per se, but not on a first date. Considering it was the love fest of the year, he didn't want a woman to get any ideas that a wedding ring was forthcoming before he got a chance to know her. So he has no choice but to wait until the whole Valentine's Day hoopla was over, then he would make his move on a sister in his church he can't take his eyes off of. For the past two years and counting, Valerie Hart hasn't been the recipient of a romantic Valentine's Day dinner invitation. To fill the void, Valerie keeps herself busy with God's business, hoping the Lord will send her perfect mate soon. Unfortunately, with no prospects in sight, it looks like that won't happen again this year. *A Woman After David's Heart* is a Valentine romance novella that can be enjoyed with or without a box of chocolates.

MAKING LOVE WORK SERIES

A Mother's Love. To Jillian Carter, it's bad when her own daughter beats her to the altar. She became a teenage mother when she confused love for lust one summer. Despite the sins of her past, Jesus forgave her and blessed her to be the best Christian example for Shana. Jillian is not looking forward to becoming an empty-nester at thirty-nine. The old adage, she's not losing a daughter, but gaining a son-in-law is not comforting as she braces for a lonely life ahead. What she doesn't expect is for two men to vie for her affections: Shana's biological father who breezes back into their lives as a redeemed man and practicing Christian. Not only is Alex still goof looking, but he's willing to right the wrong he's done in the past. Not if Dr. Dexter Harris has anything to say about it. The widower father of the groom has set his sights on Jillian and he's willing to pull out all the stops to woo her. Now the choice is hers. Who will be the next mother's love?

Love At Work. How do two people go undercover to hide an office romance in a busy television newsroom? In plain sight, of course. Desiree King is an assignment editor at KDPX-TV in St. Louis, MO. She dispatches a team to wherever breaking news happens. Her focus is to stay ahead of the competition. Overall, she's easy-going, respectable, and compassionate. But when it comes to dating a fellow coworker, she refuses to cross that professional line. Award-winning investigative reporter Bryan Mitchell makes life challenging for Desiree with his thoughtful gestures, sweet notes, and support. He tries to convince Desiree that as Christians, they could show coworkers how to blend their personal and private lives without compromising their morals.

 *Words Of Love.* Call it old fashion, but Simone French was smitten with a love letter. Not a text, email, or Facebook post, but a love letter sent through snail mail. The prose wasn't the corny roses-are-red-and-violets-are-blue stuff. The first letter contained short accolades for a job well done. Soon after, the missives were filled with passionate words from a man who confessed the hidden secrets of his soul. He revealed his unspoken weaknesses, listed his uncompromising desires, and unapologetically noted his subtle strengths. Yes, Rice Taylor was ready to surrender to love. *Whew.* Closing her eyes, Simone inhaled the faint lingering smell of roses on the beige plain stationery. She had a testimony. If anyone would listen, she would proclaim that love was truly blind.

SINGLE TITLES

If I Should Die Before I Wake (My testimony). It is of the LORD's mercies that we are not consumed, because His compassions fail not. They are new every morning, great is Thy faithfulness. Lamentations 3:22-23, God's mercies are sure; His promises are fulfilled; but a dawn of a new morning is God' grace. If you need a testimony about God's grace, then If I Should Die Before I Wake will encourage your soul. Nothing happens in our lives by chance. If you need a miracle, God's got that too. Trust Him. Has it been a while since you've had a testimony? Increase your prayer life, build your faith and walk in victory because without a test, there is no testimony.

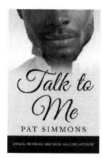

Talk to Me. Despite being deaf as a result of a fireworks explosion, CEO of a St. Louis non-profit company, Noel Richardson, expertly navigates the hearing world. What some view as a disability, Noel views as a challenge—his lack of hearing has never held him back. It also helps that he has great looks, numerous university degrees, and full bank accounts. But those assets don't define him as a man who longs for the right woman in his life. Deciding to visit a church service, Noel is blind-sided by the most beautiful and graceful Deaf interpreter he's ever seen. Mackenzie Norton challenges him on every level through words and signing, but as their love grows, their faith is tested. When their church holds a yearly revival, they witness the healing power of God in others. Mackenzie has faith to believe that Noel can also get in on the blessing. Since faith comes by hearing, whose voice does Noel hear in his heart, Mackenzie or God's?

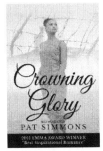

Crowning Glory. Cinderella had a prince; Karyn Wallace has a King. While Karyn served four years in prison for an unthinkable crime, she embraced salvation through Crowns for Christ outreach ministry. After her release, Karyn stays strong and confident, despite the stigma society places on ex-offenders. Since Christ strengthens the underdog, Karyn refuses to sway away from the scripture, "He who the Son has set free is free indeed." Levi Tolliver, for the most part, is a practicing Christian. One contradiction is he doesn't believe in turning the other cheek. He's steadfast there is a price to pay for every sin committed, especially after the untimely death of his wife during a robbery. Then Karyn enters Levi's life. He is enthralled not only with her beauty, but her sweet spirit until he learns about her incarceration. If Levi can accept that Christ paid Karyn's debt in full, then a treasure awaits him.

Her Dress (novella). Sometimes a woman just wants to splurge on something new, especially when she's about to attend an event with movers and shakers. Find out what happens when Pepper Trudeau is all dressed up and goes to the ball, but another woman is modeling the same attire. At first, Pepper is embarrassed, then the night gets interesting when she meets Drake Logan. *Her Dress* is a romantic novella about the all too common occurrence—two women shopping at the same place. Maybe having the same taste isn't all bad. Sometimes a good dress is all you need to meet the man of your dreams.

THE GUILTY SERIES

Guilty of Love. When do you know the most important decision of your life is the right one? Reaping the seeds from what she's sown; Cheney Reynolds moves into a historic neighborhood in Ferguson, Missouri, and becomes a reclusive. Her first neighbor, the incomparable Mrs. Beatrice Tilley Beacon aka Grandma BB, is an opinionated childless widow. Grandma BB is a self-proclaimed expert on topics Cheney isn't seeking advice—everything from landscaping to hip-hop dancing to romance. Then there is Parke Kokumuo Jamison VI, a direct descendant of a royal African tribe. He learned his family ancestry, African history, and lineage preservation before he could count. Unwittingly, they are drawn to each other, but it takes Christ to weave their lives into a spiritual bliss while He exonerates their past indiscretions.

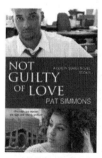

Not Guilty of Love. One man, one woman, one God and one big problem. Malcolm Jamieson wasn't the man who got away, but the man God instructed Hallison Dinkins to set free. Instead of their explosive love affair leading them to the wedding altar, God diverted Hallison to the prayer altar during her first visit back to church in years.

Malcolm was convinced that his woman had loss her mind to break off their engagement. Didn't Hallison know that Malcolm, a tenth generation descendant of a royal African tribe, couldn't be replaced? Once Malcolm concedes that their relationship can't be savaged, he issues Hallison his own edict,

"If we're meant to be with each other, we'll find our way back. If not, that means that there's a love stronger than what we had." His words begin to haunt Hallison until she begins to regret their break up, and that's where their story begins. Someone has to retreat, and God never loses a battle.

Still Guilty. Cheney Reynolds Jamieson made a choice years ago that is now shaping her future and the future of the men she loves. A botched abortion left her unable to carry a baby to term, and her husband, Parke K. Jamison VI, is expected to produce heirs. With a wife who cannot give him a child, Parke vows to find and get custody of his illegitimate son by any means necessary. Meanwhile, Cheney's twin brother, Rainey, struggles with his anger over his ex-girlfriend's actions that haunt him, and their father, Dr. Roland Reynolds, fights to keep an old secret in the past.

Follow the paths of this family as they try to determine what God wants for them and how they can follow His guidance.

The Acquittal. Two worlds apart, but their hearts dance to the same African drum beat. On a professional level, Dr. Rainey Reynolds is a competent, highly sought-after orthodontist. Inwardly, he needs to be set free from the chaos of revelations that make him question if happiness is obtainable. To get away from the drama, Rainey is willing to leave the country under the guise of a mission trip with Dentist Without Borders. Will changing his surroundings really change him? If one woman can heal his wounds, then he will believe that there is really peace after the storm.

Ghanaian beauty Josephine Abena Yaa Amoah returns to Africa after completing her studies as an exchange student in St. Louis, Missouri. Although her heart bleeds for his peace, she knows she must step back and pray for Rainey's surrender to Christ in order for God to acquit him of his self-inflicted mental torture. In the Motherland of Ghana, Africa, Rainey not only visits the places of his ancestors, will he embrace the liberty that Christ's Blood really does set every man free.

THE JAMIESON LEGACY SERIES

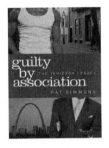

Guilty by Association. How important is a name? To the St. Louis Jamiesons who are tenth generation descendants of a royal African tribe—everything. To the Boston Jamiesons whose father never married their mother—there is no loyalty or legacy. Kidd Jamieson suffers from the "angry" male syndrome because his father was an absent in the home, but insisted his two sons carry his last name. It takes an old woman who mingles genealogy truths and Bible verses together for Kidd to realize his worth as a strong black man. He learns it's not his association with the name that identifies him, but the man he becomes that defines him.

The Guilt Trip. Aaron "Ace" Jamieson is living a carefree life. He's good-looking, respectable when he's in the mood, but his weakness is women. If a woman tries to ambush him with a pregnancy, he takes off in the other direction. It's a lesson learned from his absentee father that responsibility is optional. Talise Rogers has a bright future ahead of her. She's pretty and has no problem catching a man's eye, which is exactly what she does with Ace. Trapping Ace Jamieson is the furthest thing from Taleigh's mind when she learns she pregnant and Ace rejects her. "I want nothing from you Ace, not even your name." And Talise meant it.

Free from Guilt. It's salvation round-up time and Cameron Jamieson's name is on God's hit list. Although his brothers and cousins embraced God—thanks to the women in their lives—the two-degreed MIT graduate isn't going to let any woman take him down that path without a fight. He's satisfied with his career, social calendar, and good genes. But God uses a beautiful messenger, Gabrielle Dupree, to show him that he's in a spiritual deficit. Cameron learns the hard way that man's wisdom is like foolishness to God. For every philosophical argument he throws her way, Gabrielle exposes him to scriptures that makes him question his worldly knowledge.

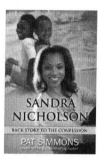

Sandra Nicholson: The Back Story. There is something to be said about a woman's first love. Kidd and Ace Jamieson's father, Samuel Jamieson broke their mother's heart. Can Sandra Nicholson recover? Her sons don't believe any man is good enough for her, especially their absentee father. Kidd doesn't deny his mother should find love again since she never married Samuel. But will she fall for a carbon copy of his father? God's love gives second chances.

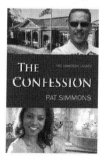

The Confession. Sandra Nicholson is a fashion consultant. Not only does she have the flair to dress her clients to impress, she catches the attention of one handsome gentleman herself. Raimond Mayfield was known as a "pretty boy" back in the day and did a lot of damage to his family. That was then. Now, Raimond's priorities are God first, business second, and restoring those broken relationships. Then he sees Sandra, and he loses sight of his goals. All he wants is a chance to get to know the beautiful woman. During their dating marathon, each soon learns they have a lot in common. That isn't a good thing once Sandra's eldest son, Kidd, gets wind of their past mistakes. Will their beloved children stand in the way of their parents' happiness?

True to the Jamieson tradition, Grandma BB is up to her shenanigans with her annual 70th birthday party, Parke and Cheney are still trying to keep her under control. Add the other Jamieson wives to the mix and there is always a happy ending. So get ready for another adventure in the Guilty series.

THE CARMEN SISTERS SERIES

Shae Carmen hasn't lost her faith in God, only the men she's come across. Shae's recent heartbreak was discovering that her boyfriend was not only married, but on the verge of reconciling with his estranged wife. Humiliated, Shae begins to second guess herself as why she didn't see the signs that he was nothing more than a devil's decoy masquerading as a devout Christian man. St. Louis Outfielder Rahn Maxwell finds himself a victim of an attempted carjacking. The Lord guides him out of harms' way by opening the gunmen's eyes to Rahn's identity. The crook instead becomes infatuated fan and asks for Rahn's autograph, and as a good will gesture, directs Rahn out of the ambush! When the news media gets wind of what happened with the baseball player, Shae's television station lands an exclusive interview. Shae and Rahn's chance meeting sets in motion a relationship where Rahn not only surrenders to Christ, but pursues Shae with a purpose to prove that good men are still out there. After letting her guard down, Shae is faced with another scandal that rocks her world. This time the stakes are higher. Not only is her heart on the line, so is her professional credibility. She and Rahn are at odds as how to handle it and friction erupts between them. Will she strike out at love again? The Lord shows Rahn that nothing happens by chance, and everything is done for Him to get the glory.

Lately, nothing in Garrett Nash's life has made sense. When two people close to the U.S. Marshal wrong him deeply, Garrett expects God to remove them from his life. Instead, the Lord relocates Garrett to another city to start over, as if he were the offender instead of the victim.

Criminal attorney Shari Carmen is comfortable in her own skin—most of the time. Being a "dark and lovely" African-American sister has its challenges, especially when it comes to relationships. Although she's a fireball in the courtroom, she knows how to fade into the background and keep the proverbial spotlight off her personal life. But literal spotlights are a different matter altogether.

While playing tenor saxophone at an anniversary party, she grabs the attention of Garrett Nash. And as God draws them closer together, He makes another request of Garrett, one to which it will prove far more difficult to say "Yes, Lord."

Landon Thomas (*In Defense of Love*) brings a new definition to the word "prodigal," as in prodigal son, brother or anything else imaginable. It's a good thing that God's love covers a multitude of sins, but He isn't letting Landon off easy. His journey from riches to rags proves to be humbling and a lesson well learned.

Real Estate Agent Octavia Winston is a woman on a mission, whether it's God's or hers professionally. One thing is for certain, she's not about to compromise when it comes to a Christian mate, so why did God send a homeless man to steal her heart?

Minister Rossi Tolliver (*Crowning Glory*) knows how to minister to God's lost sheep and through God's redemption, the game changes for Landon and Octavia.

EVERY WOMAN NEEDS A PRAYING MAN

On the surface, Brecee Carmen has nothing in common with Adrian Cole. She is a pediatrician certified in trauma care; he is a transportation problem solver for a luxury car dealership (a.k.a., a car salesman). Despite their slow but steady attraction to each other, neither one of them are sure that they're compatible. To complicate matters, Brecee is the sole unattached Carmen when it seems as though everyone else around her—family and friends—are finding love, except her.

Through a series of discoveries, Adrian and Brecee learn that things don't happen by coincidence. Generational forces are at work, keeping promises, protecting family members, and perhaps even drawing Adrian back to the church. For Brecee and Adrian, God has been hard at work, playing matchmaker all along the way for their paths cross at the right time and the right place.

Check out my fellow African American Christian fiction authors writing about faith, family and love. You won't be disappointed!

www.blackchristianreads.com